Charming Disguises

A Regina Grant Mystery

By Ngozi T. Robinson

I AM Publications

Charming Disguises

I AM Publications

(617) 564-1060
contact@iampubs.com
www.iampubs.com

Cover art by Soda Khan

ISBN: 978-1-943382-25-5

Morning After Murder

Hard light hits bodies lying haphazardly around the great room, as if they simply dropped where they stood. Mornings after are always rough on adults. Slowly, people come to life, as if the room is taking a big inhalation.

Regina leans against a doorway to the room, surveying last night's damage. She can't understand people who sleep in their clothes if they have a choice. When she had one too many mojitos last night and her energy flagged, far earlier than the rest of the partygoers, she had the sense to go to her room.

They are in a certified mansion, after all. What is anyone's excuse for sleeping all willy-nilly like this? Is this how the rich and famous do it? Regina had, unfortunately, been too uptight in college to party much, so maybe this is just how it is. She shrugs.

Regina ducks into the kitchen to see if she can rustle herself up a cheesy egg and is taken aback. The kitchen is a quiet hum of established efficiency. It seems not *all* in the house are asleep. Four people move around in livery wear (she thinks that's what they're called on those historical dramas on the BBC) in an easy, practiced fashion. They are well into preparing what looks like breakfast for an army.

A woman with a no-nonsense air doesn't stop working the griddle as she says, "Breakfast in ten, ma'am."

Regina mutters her thanks and backs out of the

kitchen. It seems that's not the place for her, either.

Breakfast brings the people fully to life, and Regina is in wonder at the whole situation. Of course, they are too rich to just line up for a buffet like they are at the Hilton. Regina tells herself she can get used to this, but it *will* take some getting used to, as the staff takes food orders from everyone. Some fantastical requests are spoken around the table, but five or ten minutes later, mouthwatering dishes that are beyond food art appear before them.

She feels like a bum because she just wants a cheesy egg, nothing fancy. And maybe some home fries. The woman who takes her order helps her out by suggesting a fruit plate in addition.

"And perhaps an international flight of toasts?" the woman continues.

Does Regina stick out here *that* much? However she comes by help, she takes it—and it *does* sound intriguing. Regina didn't even know there was such a thing as a flight of breads, but now that she knows, it's like she's been longing for it her whole life—so she agrees. She has to bite her tongue to keep from adding a cheese plate to her order. There was no need to be greedy, even if she *did* want to lick everyone else's plate. She will wait patiently for hers and be grateful for what she gets.

Conversations are still few and hushed. It seems the effects of last night weigh heavy for most. Even though Regina doesn't have a hangover, she too senses there is something harsh and brittle about the morning.

"Shall we take in the air? A turn or two around the grounds to get the day going?" Linda breaks the silence of the breakfast room as she directs her question loudly to Regina.

"Sure," Regina answers a lot more quietly and pushes herself away from the table. It is too stuffy in here.

"All this could be yours!" Linda spreads her arms out as they walk uphill towards the pool and spa area of the grounds. "I've seen the way Roger looks at you." She takes in Regina's passive expression and changes tact. "Or don't you want that?"

Regina shakes her head. "This is a lot to get used to. This is Robin Leach-level wealth, and I'm just a regular person. I'm really not sure this is the place for me."

Linda turns around to face her and keeps pace walking backwards. It's good to be fit, Regina concedes. "Look Regina, they're just regular people, too, but with money. They party hard, but they also give generously, and my boss' organization employs thousands of people, providing good jobs. They're not aliens; they can just have anything they want."

Regina shakes her head, taking a passing glance at the scene behind Linda as she does. "I don't think..."

Regina pauses as her eyes are pulled back to something out of place. Suddenly, she sprints past Linda towards the pool. A body lies face down in the pool wearing a Robin Hood costume. Regina sees dew on the back of the body and knows there is no point in checking for life. It has been there for a while.

Regina's brain starts working again, and she turns around, trying to stop Linda from seeing what no one can protect her from. Linda lets out a piercing scream, then collapses into Regina's arms. Her lover, Captain Seafood, is dead.

Tight Collar

Six days earlier...

"I'm *done* with you." John Mathews' face twists in anger.

"Dr. Mathews, please, let's work this out." Regina knows the church can't afford to lose another tithing member. Times are tough.

"You *refuse* to cut the length of the service to accommodate me. There's nothing more to say."

"I will not accommodate your schedule when it creates problems for so many other people, but I'm not stopping you from leaving whenever you need to leave. I'm truly sorry you can't be here for the full length of service, but there has to be something we can do. Mount Hope doesn't want to lose you."

"Mount Hope won't lose *me*. We're going to lose *you*."

His eyes look victorious. That means he has already set something in motion. It isn't the first time someone here has threatened to have Regina fired, but this may be the first time they have actually *done* something about it.

Regina's spine straightens. No point in looking weak and afraid, even if that's how she feels right now.

"I love you in the Lord, Dr. Mathews, but this is not *your* church. It's *our* church. The people have voted for me to lead it. Until that changes, you and I are going to have to work together."

"Work together?" His eyes go wide in surprise. "I want you *gone*."

"Yes, but unless the plan you have in motion cooks up by tonight, we're going to remain laboring together in this vineyard a little while longer. Plots to get rid of pastors usually take a while, and we can't afford to stay dysfunctional until you either get rid of me or don't. It's not right for there to be this kind of division in the body of Christ. Even if we can't agree on the time of Sunday Service, I still want you and I to be reconciled."

Regina doesn't know until now that scoffing has an actual sound to it, because that's what John Mathews does.

"You are a child." He walks out of her office in a way that seems to carry a very final tone.

Regina looks around her office and wonders if she's about to get fired because she won't move the worship service up by half an hour. People are always willing to fight to the death over *something*. It might as well be church's start time. Taking several deep breaths, she works hard not to take it personally.

Someone yells at her at least once a month because, as pastor, everything that goes wrong is personally her fault. She works hard to remind herself that, though far from the reality, that's how many people think. And the thing about life is that something is always going wrong, so it is always a good time to blame the pastor.

Regina walks out of her office and down the hall to the administrative offices. One look at Ms. Pring's face lets her know they all heard the gist of the argument.

"Tell me," Regina mutters, anxious yet fearful of her assessment.

"If they have to choose, it won't be you who stays." Ms. Pring's eyes look apologetic but clear.

"Yeah, that's what I figure, but starting church

early means we'll have to pull the kids out of the city-wide Sunday School field trips each month and they love those. He's only thinking about himself."

"You had better start thinking about *yourself* and line up some allies ready to go to bat for you on this."

"I don't want this to be a knock-down-drag-out thing where everyone has to take sides."

Ms. Pring looks at her as if she's a real life Pollyanna.

"No need to give me that look. I just want to do the work of the Lord, not play politics."

"Same thing, Pastor. And I need to know if you are going to fight this thing or sit in a corner by yourself singing Kum Ba Yah. I'm not sticking my neck out for nothing."

"So that's my only option? To let him drag me into some street brawl? Over what time church starts? There has to be a better way!"

"Are you going to fight for your pastorate or not?" Ms. Pring's voice is hard and cuts through Regina's illusions.

She sets her face, straightens her spine, and responds, "Well, I don't hear any fat lady singing. I'm fighting, I'm fighting... I just..."

"Stop looking for a peace that doesn't exist and *win*." Ms. Pring returns to work at her desk. Apparently, the issue is no longer open for discussion.

"Yes, ma'am. I need a pick-me-up; I'll pop into children's choir rehearsal for a bit. There's nothing like cute little baby angels singing off key for what ails you."

"You know Director Jones doesn't like distractions," Ms. Pring pipes up.

Regina waves a hand dismissively. "She won't even know I'm there." She walks toward the sanctuary carrying a bag of complicated emotions.

Donna Grimes, the part-time admin-assistant, steps into view from another part of the office. "Is she trying to gain two enemies in one day?"

"Looks like it." Ms. Pring shakes her head.

Regina's hopes to slip into the sanctuary unnoticed are ruined when she knocks over a ladder obstructing the door, but then she saves it from crashing into the pews almost like she planned it. It is *not* a quiet entrance.

She slowly sits down in a pew in the sanctuary's rear and lets out a sigh of relief that she can settle down with no further noise or disturbance.

Ms. Jones is the buxom, full-figured woman who serves as the church's minister of music. An accomplished musician and singer in her own right, Ms. Jones has whipped their choir into one of the best in the area, which was saying something, considering all the mega-churches in the suburbs there were to contend with.

Ms. Jones has a first name, but no one ever uses it, not even in print. Ms. Jones is a diva, and everyone knows not to disturb or disrupt her.

She stares at Regina with her hands on her hips, head shaking in disapproval and eyes latched onto her soul. Regina puts up her hands to show she comes in peace, and Ms. Jones finally turns her attention back to the children. The pianist plays a melody and all the children straighten up, swaying from side-to-side in unison.

Regina closes her eyes and listens to the children sing one of her favorite hymns.

"You may build great cathedrals large or small, "you can build skyscrapers grand and tall,

"you may conquer all the failures of the past,
"but only what you do for Christ will last."

Regina closes her eyes and tries to enjoy the
song, but she has to admit it's hard. The kids are
hesitant and the words seem to die before they've begun
to live. The notes are all over the place. She is relieved
this is all Ms. Jones' problem and not her own.

She notices Nevin sitting at the end of her pew
and scoots over—in the smoothest way she can, so as
not to disturb Ms. Jones' concentration—to the little
boy. He is at that age, seven if her memory serves her
right, that is all elbows and knees.

"Hi, Nevin," she says in a voice pitched so only
he can hear it.

"Humph." He draws his knees to his chest.

"Aren't you supposed to be up there with the
other kids?"

"Sort of." He pulls his shirt collar until his head
is buried in his shirt.

"You *know* I want to know what *that* means.
What's the scoop?"

Nevin lets out a little laugh. "You are weird,
Pastor Grant."

"Shhh. Don't tell anyone. I think I've got them all
fooled." They share a chuckle. "What's up?"

Nevin's smile drops, and he makes a study of his
shoes as he kicks them back and forth. "Ms. Jones said I
can't sing with my friends because of me having tune
deafness. I haven't told my ma yet, so she's still been
dropping me off here on Tuesdays. I'm not supposed to
be here."

Regina's heart breaks.

"I'm sorry, Nevin. Do you want me to be with you
when your mom picks you up today to help you tell her
what's going on?"

His legs kick the air a little faster. "I guess."

"Good. Things will get better. I'm sure Ms. Jones will find the perfect way for you to be involved. You know she loves you, right? We all do!" She puts an arm around Nevin and gives him a hug.

"No, she doesn't! She said no one wants to hear me sing. Pastor, do I really sound that bad so I can't sing with my brother and my friends?"

Regina counts to ten, breathes, and blinks the red she sees out of her vision. If Nevin's account is accurate, it seems Ms. Jones has crushed the boy's spirit. The truth is Nevin sounds like a cat in heat when he sings. It is well and truly awful, yet she looks forward to the joy on his face every time.

She has to talk to Ms. Jones, but it has to be relaxed. Regina is at least smart enough to know she can't fight two battles at once and come out ahead. As much as Regina wants to go after Ms. Jones, she knows that two fires only make a bigger fire. She had to find a way to love Ms. Jones instead of wanting to rip her to shreds.

Looking down into the eyes of a little boy who just wants to know why he can't sing with the others, she is reminded it's not about her.

"Well, Nevin. You want the truth, or something that sounds good?"

"Something that sounds good!"

"*Really*?"

"The truth, I guess then."

"OK," Regina turns to give Nevin her full attention. "You're not the best singer in terms of ability, but you're one of the best in terms of joy, hands down. The nice thing about the church is that we don't have to act like the rest of the world and only be interested in winning prizes and contests trying to be perfect.

"God appreciates your singing even more than I do. And besides, whenever we offer something to God with a sincere heart, Jesus cleans it up and gift wraps it for us. So, I guarantee you, you sound better than a choir of angels to God when you sing."

"Wow, I must sound really bad because you were trying really hard."

Children can be annoying little oracles.

"I just want to make sure you understand *I* love your singing, even though I won't be suggesting you go on American Idol soon. Is that still a thing?"

"Yeah."

"I know one thing Ms. Jones cares about, besides *you*, is the excellence of the group. I imagine it must be very hard for her to balance everyone's needs. She still loves you loads, though."

"I guess."

It isn't a ringing endorsement, but Regina has to soften some of his hurt with Ms. Jones. She will take 'I guess' for now.

As Regina turns back to face forward, she is surprised to see Ms. Jones standing over her. She might as well be breathing fire.

"I should have known I couldn't turn my back on you." Ms. Jones' arms cross over her ample bosom.

"What?" Regina is confused.

"Yes, I cut him from the choir. What, did you bring him here to confront me?"

"Ms. Jones, I think there's some confusion here."

Her eyes go from Regina to the boy and back again. "Right. Because I'm *that* dumb."

'You just *may* be,' Regina thinks, then chides herself immediately. "Maybe we could start over?" She can not make another enemy today.

"Just stay out of my way," she huffs before making a point of turning her back on Regina. She marches back to the choir loft, where the children are thoroughly goofing off.

"Wow," Nevin says. "Does she love you, too?"

Children.

"Of course, But I *am* in trouble."

"Oh, boy. I don't want to be you!" Nevin laughs.

"What? You won't trade with me? I thought we were friends?!"

Nevin rolls on his side with laughter. Apparently, she is hilarious. Ms. Jones leers at them over the disturbance, and Regina raises her hands in apology. She is on thin ice, and that doesn't change the fact that she still has to talk to Ms. Jones about Nevin. Regina has *defended* her, only to wind up on the receiving end of her wrath.

That's it, Regina calls it a day. She has nothing left to give to anyone, not even herself. She wants to go home to her tiny house on wheels in the church parking lot, hug her cat, crawl into bed, pull the covers over her head, and ignore the world.

But she has told Ms. Pring she will fight, so it is probably time to start doing that. Walking back to the administrative offices, she presents herself in front of Ms. Pring's desk. In a voice that she hopes isn't too pathetic, she asks, "How do I fight this?"

Ms. Pring and Ms. Grimes descend on her, and the air takes on a conspiratorial tone. They push a piece a paper toward her. "We made a list. You need to get support from at least eight of these fourteen people."

Regina looks over the list. It makes sense. "How do I get their support?"

"We made another list." They are enjoying this way too much. "Here are a few things each of them wants. Give them something."

Regina reviews the second list. Most of it is stuff she thinks she can live with. Her eyebrows raise several times as she sees some of the items. "Some of these..."

"That's blackmail. In case."

"And *this* is how to keep a church?" She lets out a sigh of frustration.

"You can't fight this fight *and* fight the rules at the same time. You have to decide if you want it bad enough. Do you want to keep this church or not?"

Bright Lights, Big City

"I *will* not." Regina puts the phone call on speaker and leans back in her chair.

"You will *too*."

"See, I feel sorry for you, Nephew, that's all this is. If you won't come to me, I suppose that means I have to come to you, even if it is in New York City. That place has broken more hearts than the ace of spades, *plus* there are too many people, *plus* a speed limit of 55 on highways? But I digress. I can't wait to come see you."

"Aunt Regina, you will have a good time, I promise. I just know you would love this city if you gave it a chance. It has captured *my* heart."

"I rather think that has more to do with the company than the geography, Jonathan. How is Ilana?"

"She's looking forward to meeting you. I was telling her about our big reunions when we were kids. Now, it seems like we are dwindling down. So, yes, come and prove to her I have people."

"Then people you shall have," Regina says gallantly. "How hard do you want me to go on her? Should I break her?" Her voice has a serious tone to it.

"You *do* know that you being my aunt is purely a technicality, don't you? We are only a few years apart."

"Sounds like you're trying to get out of nephew duty to me."

"Don't you think we're a little old for this?"

"Oh, no, no. Nephew duty is very serious. You *must* deliver the tea brewed at the correct temperature or all the realm will be lost."

"I'm a grown man now."

"Still a nephew."

"Alright, alright. I'll be on nephew duty. Just please show up on time. I know how you are. We'll have a great time, I promise."

"Oh, I'll just be happy to see you... and, to be honest, I could use a bit of a break."

"Pastor work got you down?"

"Not down, but definitely exhausted. A Sunday away will be good for what ails me."

"Uh, oh. Who do I have to beat up?"

"I love you, nephew. It's good to know there's somebody in my corner on sight. It does me a lot of good right now."

"Hmm. I don't like it. Make your visit sooner rather than later. I want to lay eyes on you and make my *own* determination."

"Sounds like a plan."

The Acela train—she missed the regular train's departure by *this* much—is smooth and pulls into Grand Central Station in downtown New York City only a little later than scheduled. She steps off the train and is disappointed that the platform is not swirling with smoke and mysterious people, like in the old movies she favors. The moment is brief, because she sees her nephew and snaps back to the reason she is here: family.

"Jonathan!" She squeezes him tight, remembering what it is like to be around family in a powerful way. She steps back and takes him in. "Let me look at you. FaceTime is just not the same."

Jonathan pulls her hands away. "Auntie, stop inspecting me like I'm a specimen. Yes, I'm nice and healthy, no signs of jaundice or croup. Leave me be, now."

"Ok, ok, I can be cool." Regina notices his companion and realizes the source of his embarrassment. She hadn't meant to treat him like a child in front of his lady. Regina sticks out a hand to her in welcome. "You must be Ilana. It's so nice to meet you."

Ilana opens her arms and hugs Regina. "I've heard so much about you. It's great to finally meet you!"

"Oh! Thank you, dear." Regina makes a face, asking for help from Jonathan as Ilana tosses her side-to-side in the fiercest bear hug she has ever experienced. Jonathan just laughs.

"Ilon, let's not overwhelm her. It was hard enough to get her to come in the first place." He gently untangles Ilana from her embrace.

"Sorry, I'm a hugger!" Ilana laughs and almost gives her another hug before she catches herself.

"Ok, let's get you out of Grand Central and to our first meeting!" Jonathan rubs his hands together.

"Meeting? I'm on vacation! Who do I even have to meet in New York City?"

Ilana and Jonathan share a look.

"I think you should make an exception for this," Jonathan says.

"What have you gotten me into, nephew?" She gives him a wary look.

He shrugs, "What can I say? I guess it runs in the family." His Cheshire cat grin, still way too cute for a grown man, makes it hard to be mad at him.

"Let's do it," she says in happy resignation.

"That's my auntie!" He puts an arm around her as they walk. "Never met a challenge she didn't say yes to."

Making their way outside, Jonathan hails a cab

for them. "Head to Wall Street," he directs the driver.

"Wall Street?" Regina's face becomes serious. "I am *not* dressed for Wall Street."

"Do you even know what the dress code *is* for Wall Street?"

"I know it's where fancy people go in boring but expensive suits. None of that is me."

"We're playing against type. This will be refreshing for them." Jonathan speaks casually, as if there's no import to his words.

"I've played exceedingly nice with all of this, but when are you going to tell me what's going on?" Regina asks.

Suddenly, Jonathan looks like he did when he was eight years old and had taken her bike for a spin without her permission, only to crash it in the ditch.

"That bad, huh?"

"I submitted your name for a job and you are on the short list to fill a new role as chaplain for the Securities and Exchange Commission. We're going now to meet the head decision maker, who is rooting for you." The words pour out of Jonathan in a rush.

Regina stares at him. And stares. And stares. "You've lost your mind."

"I know you're not *happy* lately where you are. I know having to upgrade to the Acela so you would only be fashionably late was not a financial decision you could make easily. You're living in a tiny house on wheels in the church parking lot, for goodness' sake! So, I did some investigating. Turns out the SEC is hungering for someone just like you, someone real with faith and no judgment. Just come and meet Roger, who's already in your corner, and talk about it. It just might be the answer you're looking for."

Regina gets ready to give her nephew a good dressing down, then stops and deflates. "Maybe you see things clearer than I do about my situation. And it sounds like you did a lot of work on my behalf. From the way you two are grinning, I'm guessing you did too, Ilana. So, thank you both. If you're sure, the least I can do is take a meeting and find out more about this whole thing."

Jonathan and Ilana celebrate the good news with a high five.

As their cab wound its way to Wall Street, the buildings get taller and more ornate. They drive right by the bull and little girl bronze statues made famous by this place, and Regina plasters her face to the window like the tourist she is. Finally, the cab drops them off in front of a sleek building so tall she can't guess the number of floors.

"This person has an office here?" Regina is feeling intimidated all over again.

"Roger owns the building." Jonathan sees the color drain from Regina's face and rushes to reassure her. "But, he is super down to earth, you'll love him. Tell her, hon."

Ilana pipes in. "Yes, he's my boss and believe me, he's just dying to meet you. He's your biggest fan, really."

"Don't tell me you're *afraid*?" Jonathan arches an eyebrow at her.

Regina's eyes cut to him, and she straightens her spine. "Of course not. Let's do this." She *is* afraid of someone who could own an entire building like this, but she won't give anyone the satisfaction of knowing that.

They take an elevator up to the top floor. Regina thinks she has never been in a building this tall before. Eighty floors is hard for her to conceptualize.

They are ushered onto the Moile Enterprises executive floor. They needed a guard's security card to get access. The elevator doors open, and it feels like they're transported to a chic hotel lobby. There's art on the walls that is too abstract to be cheap. Regina tries not to shrink in the presence of so many fine and expensive things.

A pleasant young man makes a beeline to greet them. "Ilana, Jonathan, so good to see you." He turns his gaze to Regina. "And you must be Reverend Grant. It is an honor to meet you, pastor. How was the trip up here? Can I get you anything?"

Regina takes a moment to take in the man's mile-a-minute speaking style and translate it into a normal person's pace. "I would *love* a cup of chamomile tea. I don't suppose you have any?"

The man smiles as if hers is a charming question. "Of course, pastor. Just one moment." He types something into a tablet and turns his attention back to them. "Let me take you into Mr. Moile's reception area, where you can wait in comfort."

Walking them across the lounge area, he opens two ornately carved doors, then steps back for them to enter. The new room is almost as large as the lounge area, but it is more sparsely decorated, making it look cavernous.

Regina lightly runs her fingers along a beautiful green vase when Jonathan whispers in her ear. "Your big fat fingers have skin oils that can damage the surface, genius." She casually removes her hand from the vase as if it's her idea.

The place seems far too elegant and selective to tolerate Regina in her jeans and sweater. She should have put down her foot about not being dressed appropriately. At least folks here seem to have enough etiquette not to notice or make an issue out of it.

An older woman is stationed on a wall that is the one part of the room that looks like an office. She looks up from her work and spares them a brief smile.

"That's Eunice," Ilana says in a low voice. "She's Roger's executive assistant."

"I'm getting a very, 'I am not to be trifled with,' vibe," Regina whispers back. Ilana nods her head solemnly. Regina half means it as a joke, but takes it as forewarning at Ilana's response.

"These are the forms the SEC will need to process your clearance. Many of them are quite detailed. You will want to get started immediately." Eunice deposits a healthy-sized folder in Regina's lap before returning to her command station.

Regina looks at the thick pile. "Am I trying to get into the CIA here?"

"It's standard." Jonathan dismisses her concerns. "You're going to have access to some of the most important people in the country. They just want to make sure you don't secretly owe a bookie a billion dollars."

"I owe my veterinarian. Reginald ate a mouse. It did not go well, but that's about it. A waste of trees to tell them that."

"Just let Roger explain it all. I think this could really be a perfect fit for you. Simmer down and give it a chance."

Regina opens her mouth to speak, but then her brain catches up with her words and she reconsiders. "I am really trying to keep an open mind."

"We'd be in the same city! How great would that be?"

"*That's* the downside for me; so many people in this city of broken dreams, all in a hurry."

"That's what you're the antidote for! Think of how much good you could do."

Regina thinks about the possibilities and likes what she sees.

"You can see it, can't you?"

She brings her attention back to the present. "Maybe. I'm *here*. I'll give it a chance, I promise."

"That's great. You'll love Roger, I just know it."

A tall man enters abruptly and walks by them as if they aren't there. Regina takes in a handsome man of honey-brown complexion, well-muscled, and with a distinguishing streak of white through his close cut black hair. Everything about him looks like he stepped off the cover of GQ magazine. She curses her travel wear.

Eunice gestures towards the three of them and the man glances at them before shaking his head and heading towards another door, presumably his office. Ilana swiftly intersects him.

"Mr. Moile, hi. We have Reverend Regina Grant here, as you requested. We've been telling her how excited you are to meet her."

Regina has to give it to Ilana. She doesn't take no for an answer, but steps up when she needs to. That's a big plus in her book. It looks like her nephew has made a good choice. She hadn't doubted it, but it is still nice to see evidence of it.

"Not now, 'Lana. Have Eunice schedule something."

"We *are* scheduled, sir, for now."

Roger takes a deep breath, takes off his glasses and pinches the bridge of his nose.

"I can't meet with you now. Something's come up. And, when we do reschedule," his eyes turn to Regina, "perhaps you would consider wearing something more appropriate."

Roger's words hit her like a blow in an already tender spot, but she wastes no time recovering. "You should try some valerian root tea for your sleeplessness."

Roger, who has already turned his back to them,

pauses and turns around. "What?"

"The circles around the eyes and slightly pallid complexion. I assume that's from you not sleeping. You should try some valerian root. A good night's sleep will do your attitude a world of good." She delivers the last line flatly and levels her eyes at him.

Roger looks confused, as if he doesn't understand the criticism, which, in Regina's opinion, is incredibly mild. There was no need for him to have commented on her attire unless he wanted to shame her. That makes him a small man to her. But maybe his behavior can be corrected for the next person he runs across who doesn't meet his expectations.

"OK," Roger says sheepishly and to no one in particular. Turning on his heels, he leaves the room.

Eunice spares them a look of regret before returning to her computer screen.

Regina rounds on her nephew. "If that is someone being in my corner, I hate to see who's against me!" She shakes her head and collects her purse, preparing to leave. "You are taking me away from here and providing me with some of this oft-mentioned 'fun' immediately, if you know what's good for you."

She smiles as if what Roger said hadn't hurt as much as it did. She knows none of this is Jonathan's fault and is eager to relieve him of any guilt he might feel.

Jonathan returns her smile, eventually."Yes, you're right. You came here to have a good time and I mean for you to have *two* of 'em."

"He's not normally like this. I'm mortified and so sorry!" Ilana has a look of apology on her face.

"Both of you, it's *OK*. These things happen, I guess they *must*, right? Because it certainly just happened to me. But really, he was right. I'm *not* dressed for the occasion, which, from the looks of it, is plotting to take over the world." She looks again at the luxury of her surroundings. "Let's just call it 'one of those things' and get out of here. I'm in the mood for Italian. New Yorkers have strong opinions on that. I want to weigh in!"

She smiles and animates as they discuss dinner options. The part of her that had dared to hope in any of this will keep until she is alone and can lick her wounds carefully and in peace. She had been weighed and found wanting. While it is over a little thing like her attire, it still doesn't feel good to be judged as not good enough. If she never sees Roger Moile again, it will be too soon.

All's Fair In Love and...

Regina stays out way too late, making Jonathan and Ilana take her to multiple tea houses and food destinations she had researched.

"Ooh, are we near the Bronx? I heard about this great dessert bar."

"Auntie, where do you put it? You have just about eaten your way across this city. I'm this close to unbuttoning my pants!"

"Ha, I know your manners are too good for that. Are you really *that* full?" Her eyes say pretty please and she smiles in what she hopes is an ingratiating manner.

Jonathan sighs and looks at Ilana. "You got one more stop in you?"

"Oh, she wants to make a good impression on me. Of course she does." Regina hooks an arm through each of theirs and almost skips down the street at the thought of gelato handmade like they do in "the old country."

"Nobody would guess you don't like New York City by the way you're acting, you know." Jonathan hails a cab.

"Oh, believe me, my introverted self is going to need significant time to recover from this trip. But, as long as it's for a little while, let's go nuts and paint the town red!"

"Watch out, Auntie, I'm gonna show you some parts of the City that will totally win you over."

"I appreciate you, Jonathan. Even though the job that you totally masterminded behind my back didn't work out, I still love that you thought enough of me to do something like that. *And* I love you for letting me geek out on tea and food."

"Love you, too, Aunt Regina." They share a hug, then he puts an arm around Ilana. "Love you, three." He kisses her on the nose.

"You two are the cutest. You let me know it's possible. I might actually get there one of these days."

At the gelato place, Regina places a hand on her happy belly. The only thing that can make it better is the perfect cup of exotic tea. She scrolls through her phone for possibilities when Ilana clears her throat.

"Don't be mad at me, but Roger really wants to apologize to you." Ilana looks sheepish.

"Why did you have to bring him up? We're having a good time here."

"Because he's on his way here now."

"You told him where we were?" Regina feels like she's been tattled on.

"He already knew—he always knows—I just wanted to give you a heads up."

"It's three in the morning. Good people are home in bed!"

Jonathan and Ilana give her pointed 'then what does that make you?' looks that hit home.

"*I* am in the middle of a glorious adventure exploring the food and drink of New York City. It's different. Besides, I'm grown, I'm not hurting anybody. I can stay out as long as I want." She sticks her tongue out to emphasize her maturity.

That's when Roger Moile locks eyes with her from the creamery's entrance. He walks toward her and Regina feels pinned down by his gaze. Gone is the tailored suit and tie he had worn earlier. He looks equally at home in the brown slacks and tan suede blazer. He looks better than she does in her attire, *and* he's dressed for the occasion.

He brings a small bouquet out from behind his back and presents it to Regina. "I owe you a big apology."

"Is this how business is done in New York City?"

Roger winces. "I completely deserve that. There is no excuse for my behavior. I meant to welcome you and be your champion in getting this position, and I failed at that. I ask you for another chance."

"My champion? You don't even know me."

"That's not *entirely* true. You and I just met today, but Ilana has filled me in, and I've seen several of your sermons online. I feel like I know you. Please give me a chance to truly make up for my inexcusable behavior."

'He knows how to turn on the charm,' Regina thinks as she looks into his chestnut eyes. Her shoulders drop and she relaxes in his presence. She can see him notice the change in her body language as his smile gets more confident.

"Have a seat and join us for some amazing gelato." She smiles at him and forgives him for her hurt feelings, but keeps in mind that this man definitely has two faces.

"While I'm sure this gelato is great, there's a little hole in the wall I know that has better. Want me to call and have them open up?"

Regina looks at him as if he's grown a second head. "It's three in the morning. Good people are home in bed!"

Roger raises an eyebrow at her, and Jonathan and Ilana laugh.

"Oh, you two are no help!" Regina laughs at herself. "What I mean to say is, if they're closed, don't bother them. I can go when they're open."

"Or *we* could go right now, unless you're afraid

your gelato won't hold a candle to mine. And don't worry, I know you're into fair trade and all that. Believe me, I will more than fairly compensate the Balducci's for their time. We can talk about the job."

Regina makes a face like he just assigned homework at the mention of job talk.

"Or not."

Regina thinks it would be like a movie, having some place open up just for her.

"Well, if you're sure they won't mind and they'll be fairly paid, why not?"

"*Generously* paid," Roger comments.

"I stand corrected." She looks at Jonathan and Ilana. "You two ready to ride?" She can see Ilana has put on a more professional demeanor in the presence of her employer.

"Of course," Ilana answers cheerfully, as if it's a completely normal suggestion.

Roger takes an assessing look at Ilana. "Not many people stand up to me like you did earlier. I value that. Let's talk next week about how I can reward that spine of yours."

Ilana's smile grows both wider and shyer somehow.

"Great, I'll call a ride share," Regina announces.

Roger scoffs. "My car's outside."

As they head outside, Regina guesses that his "car" is the black Escalade limo double parked in front.

"*That's* your car?" Regina can't help that her jaw drops. She hasn't been in a limousine since she did a tour of the Las Vegas Strip with her girlfriends a few years ago. It was nowhere as sleek, or as casually used as this one.

Roger pauses at the back door of the limo, waves away the driver who gets out to open the door, and turns to Regina, a serious look on his face.

"I'm wealthy, and I won't apologize for it. Understand, I have worked hard and built everything I have. I'd like to think I do a lot of good with what I've been blessed with. Give me a chance to show you who I really am."

He looks so sincere that Regina feels a twinge of guilt for judging him unfairly. "I was just saying it's fancy, is all." Regina reminds herself not to be defensive when she gets caught in an unflattering light. She lifts her eyes to meet his. "I'll be honest, you live in a different world. It's disorienting."

"I live in a different world, but there's more than one way to be wealthy. Let me show you *my* way. If you get this job, you're going to have to deal with life on a very different level and the income and access that will come with it. Might as well try it on for size."

Regina is impressed with his statement, she admits. Not everything different and new is bad or suspect, right? She takes a deep breath in and exhales her confusion and hesitation away.

"Show me your world, then." The look in her eyes says she's ready for the challenge.

Roger opens the door and she, Jonathan, and Ilana get in. Roger walks to the driver's door to discuss something with him.

"Quick, how much does this job pay?" Regina whispers.

Jonathan looks embarrassed. "A little over a million," he mumbles.

"Jonathan, why on earth do you look ashamed?" Ilana can't understand his behavior.

Regina understands completely.

"It is hard for a rich man to get into heaven," Regina and Jonathan recite in unison.

"Oh, come on, you can't be serious." Ilana looks back and forth between them in disbelief. "Think of the good you could do with that salary, with that position."

"I *am* thinking about it... but the love of money is the root of many evils. There's temptation there, too."

"Give Roger a chance to show you wealth doesn't have to be a trap. He is not like that. I *know* you know it's possible to be rich *and* good."

"Of course I do. It's just easier *not* to be rich and good." Regina laughs at herself. "Oh, this conversation is far too theological for my vacation. I'm here to experience it all with an open mind."

"*And* a full belly. I would have worn different clothes if I had known you were going to force feed us like this." Jonathan half jokes and half complains.

"Oh, poor baby," Ilana says sweetly.

"You two," Regina laughs.

Roger opens the door and joins them. "Great, you already have the party going. We're all set, they're opening up for us and we should be eating your choice of gelato in half an hour."

"Gelato!" Regina smiles as she shouts out and gets hungry all over again.

As they ride off into the not quite yet morning, Regina thinks, 'This really *is* the city that never sleeps.'

Cozy

The "Escalade Gang," as Regina insists on calling them, goes for gelato that she has to admit is the best she has ever tasted. They sit around the table digesting their food, as even Regina finally has to admit she's stuffed.

"You know, it's almost time for breakfast," Roger notes.

Objections pour out of their mouths at the thought of one more bite of food.

"No," Regina says flatly.

"You've got to be kidding me!" Jonathan looks like a sleepy child as he protests.

"I don't think I can manage, sir." Ilana gently tries to get out of it.

Roger laughs as he takes them in. "No seconds, then?"

A small, thin Italian woman comes out from behind the cafe's counter. She has one of those faces where Regina can't tell if she's 60 or 100.

"Did somebody say seconds?" She carefully deposits a small confectionary in front of each of them.

Regina stifles a moan at the appearance of more food.

"You treat us too well, Noni," Roger says.

"Of course! You are like my own child. You and that hard head." She raps him on the head with a hand, then affectionately puts an arm around him. "You usually come alone, just your thoughts and all the pistachio gelato we can scoop. It does my heart good to see you with friends, and such attractive ones." She lifts an eyebrow and eyes Regina pointedly.

"Oh, no, it's not like that at all. We just met today," Regina rushes to correct the woman.

Roger gives Regina a look she can't interpret.

"The first date and you have her out until 5am? You don't do anything by halves, ha ha!" The woman punches Roger in the shoulder.

Regina wants to correct her again, but the woman's smile and demeanor are too infectious to resist.

"He threatened me with the best gelato I've ever had. How could I resist?" Regina joins in with the woman's laughter, and soon they are all smiles and jokes at the table.

"Now," the woman announces, "get out of my shop. You never sleep, Roger. How many times do I have to tell you to take care of yourself, my child?"

"Maybe one of these days, Noni."

He takes her hand, and they enjoy a moment of quiet reflection together. Regina sees a relationship that money can't buy.

"You're right, it *is* time to go." Roger stands up and puts his blazer back on. "It's Saturday. That means we go to the Hamptons."

"You young people and your plans," the woman clucks. "Just as long as you get some sleep." She looks at Regina. "Take care of him for me."

Regina has a surprised and amused look on her face when she notices Roger looking at her strangely again. She stays focused.

"What do you mean 'we?'" It's Regina's turn to arch an eyebrow and stare at Roger.

"I asked to show you my world. The city and business are only part of it. The East Hamptons is where I go to get away from it all and get back to first principles. I would love for you to see it." Roger looks at Regina as he speaks and then takes in the entire group. "*All* of you, please, be my guests at Chez Moile for the weekend."

Regina blinks sleepily at him. "Can I take a nap first?" She jerks as she realizes she said that out loud.

"Of course, but I'm *not* letting you go back to that sketchy hotel you're staying at in Astoria."

Regina is confused. Glancing at Jonathan and Ilana, they shake their heads; they didn't tell him where she was staying. "Are you the Illuminati? How do you...?"

"Eunice tells me these things. I make it a point not to ask her how she knows. I have never asked her if she is the Illuminati, though. Allow me to see your things are collected and deposit you at a more appropriate venue."

"I thought it was charming, not sketchy."

Jonathan and Ileana share a look, and then say in unison, "Sketchy."

"I'll be fine." She spares them a scolding look. "Thank you for offering."

Roger gets a stern look on his face. "I know you are a strong, independent, capable Black woman, but please let me help you?"

Jonathan breaks out in laughter, "Oooh Auntie, he done told you!"

Regina throws up her hands and gives up. "This is the support I get." She takes in Jonathan laughing and Ilana pretending she's not there. "Fine. I get along with a lot of help from my friends." She stares daggers through Jonathan and Ilana.

"Are we friends, then?" Roger closes the distance between them and is suddenly too close.

Regina smells his cologne. She does not step back like a skittish girl.

"Not yet. But I will accept your application," she says coyly.

"How do I apply?" His chestnut eyes are locked on hers, and the rest of the world disappears for Regina.

"I, uh, well," she clears her throat and regains her wits, "You apply by answering this question—why were you rude to me in your office earlier? You seemed to go out of your way to call out my attire. And, yes, I *am* a strong, independent Black queen, but you still hurt my feelings."

Roger drops his head and exhales, but he doesn't step back— Regina notices. He stays engaged.

"A deal went sideways that morning because someone I thought was a friend betrayed me. Being backed into a corner doesn't make me respond well. I was mad at the world, and you were collateral damage. I saw you... I saw you, and I was mad at God for screwing me over and you are God's representative, so I lashed out. And I know it was wrong and I'm sorry. I promise you that is not how I am. I'd like the chance to make it right."

"You know, apparently, your *friend* screwed you over and not God, right?"

Roger nods. "I sure would have appreciated a heads up, though. Why doesn't God answer when I call?"

Regina hears the confusion and hurt in the question. "God seems frustratingly silent sometimes when we need God to speak the most. How do you get in touch?"

"What do you mean?"

"When you want to hear from God, what do you do?"

Roger looks perplexed.

"Are you expecting God to pop up like a jack-in-the-box with the exact information you need?"

"You make it sound silly."

"I was being a little flippant, yes, but have you ever thought that maybe God *is* speaking, but we don't know how to listen because we're waiting for some kind of obvious, genie-in-the-lamp type of response?"

"You're saying I don't know how to listen?"

"I don't know you well enough to say, Roger, but it *is* true for many people when it comes to hearing God."

Regina can see the gears turning for Roger as he digests the information. He raises his head and looks at her. "Do you accept my apology?"

"Yes. Application complete. Now we can be friends." Regina beams at him.

"You're pretty special, you know that?" Roger puts a hand on her elbow.

Regina realizes they're so close they're almost embracing... and that they are not alone. They are standing in the streets of New York as the decent people who were in bed are coming to life. And Jonathan and Ilana are here.

She steps back and reorients herself. "I believe somebody said something about the Hamptons?"

Roger seems to notice his surroundings. "Of course. 'Lana and Jonathan, a car will pick you up in three hours. Be ready. Rev. Grant, I hope you will consider coming with me."

"Just the two of us in this big thing?" She gestures to the SUV limo.

Roger laughs. "Oh no, friend, I'm driving."

"That laugh sounds a little wicked to me." She makes the sign of the cross on herself.

"Wait, you're not Catholic."

"No, but I figure I can use all the help I can get."

"I'll get you there in one piece, I promise. Ah yes, here is Arthur with the car."

A sleek, dark green Mercedes pulls up behind them. Regina assumed he would have one of those fancy car models she had never even heard of. A young man gets out of the driver's seat and tosses keys to Roger.

"We can swing by your motel..."

"Hotel," Regina corrects.

"*Motel,* and get your things, then drive out. How's that sound?"

"Roger, I haven't slept. I'm in yesterday's clothes. And, speaking of inappropriate, I *definitely* don't have clothes for the Hamptons."

"There'll be clothes waiting for you at my estate."

"Because you're a wizard?" Regina asks.

"No, but I like to prepare, *and* I have an eye for figures." He lets his gaze take her in, lingering in certain places.

"So there are magically clothes in my size just waiting for me at your *estate*?" Regina looks around in frustration that all of this seems so normal to him. Glancing at Jonathan and Ilana, she sees they are studiously trying to avoid her gaze. "Excuse me a minute."

She walks over to Jonathan and begins a whispered conversation. "Is this man going to murder me and throw me into the Hudson or something? This is *weird*, right?"

"This is *wealth*—nothing is an obstacle and things that seem weird to us are common to them. But I don't think it's murder you have to worry about. I could feel the electricity between you two during your little tête-à-tête. He's interested, and *you* don't seem to be running in the opposite direction. He's doing my work for me to get you to move to New York. Roger and Regina sitting in a tree, K-I-S-S-I..."

"You're a child." Regina shakes her head and

walks back over to Roger.

"I'm in. Let's do it."

Roger's smile is wide and genuine. "You'll enjoy this, I promise. I want you to meet some of my friends. You'll see they're real, genuine people."

Regina knows that plenty of people can act like real, genuine jerks, but she understands his point. "Well, lead on then."

Roger escorts her to the car and opens the door for her, something she's not used to. Roger has to beat her hand to the door handle.

"*Let* me help you," he says pointedly.

Regina steps back and lets him open the door.

"Let me show you how you should be treated. I'm sorry, but not sorry, that it seems you don't already have a man around to treat you like you deserve."

He shuts her door and walks around to the driver's side. Regina sees Jonathan and Ilana staring at her with their eyebrows raised and mischievous grins on their faces.

Roger gets in and adjusts the seat. "You ready?"

Regina smiles at him. "I'm ready. Show me your world."

The Hamptons sounds like a dream come true. She can hardly imagine being in such a place, rubbing elbows with the rich and famous. It could be the trip of a lifetime. This potential job and Roger—she has to admit he is growing on her—might just be the answer to all her problems.

Rarified Air

Once they get out of the city, the weather is nice enough that Roger lowers the top of the convertible and they drive with the wind in their hair for much of the way.

He takes his eyes off the road for a moment to look at Regina. "This is so good for me. It's been too long since I got away from it all. I feel I can breathe out here in a way that I can't in the city."

"I'm just trying to figure out how you're still awake," Regina half-jokes. He seems thankfully, though mysteriously, awake and alert for someone who hasn't slept in over a day.

"Sleep is hard for me sometimes. I just roll with it."

"But you should still be tired. Is this manic behavior?"

Roger's face takes on a hard look, and his body tenses. Then he takes a slow breath in and out. "I don't talk about that."

"I am *so* sorry. I can't believe I just blurted that out." Regina squirms uncomfortably in her seat from the guilt of being flippant.

"I don't talk about this," he repeated.

Regina sees hurt in him and cannot leave well enough alone. "But you *could*, if you wanted to, to me. Just an openhanded offer. I won't be offended if you decline."

Roger stays silent, and Regina is about to grab her phone for company when he clears his throat.

"I have guilt from my past... sometimes, there's no point in trying to sleep. But I'm still running, even when I'm awake."

"Have you done all you can to make amends for whatever happened?"

"Yes," he says emphatically. "I absolutely have. But it still happened."

"Do you want to tell me about it?"

Roger gives her another long look. "I was in a land development deal many years ago. Unbeknownst to me, my partners were buying substandard building materials and pocketing the money. All those people in Unit 62 buried in the rubble of their own homes. 12 people—three children—perished. I can't bring back life, so I can't make it right. Once again, your Big Guy in the sky isn't doing me any favors."

"You think that story is about you? Are you really more upset that God put you in that situation than that those people died?"

"Hold on, I didn't mean it that way."

Regina takes a breath and tries not to get sentimental about the loss of life. It barely works. "How did you mean it?"

"I thought God was supposed to help his children, help *me*, but I've never felt more alone than when that happened. I can't count on Him." Roger keeps his eyes on the road.

"I hear you saying it's awful to feel alone. Are there any times when you *do* feel God's presence filling that space?"

"When I was a kid, I used to get so excited on Sunday mornings. Mamma always made sure I had a suit that fit so I could go to church. I felt like God and I got to have a party every week. Then I grew up. He doesn't talk to me anymore." Roger downshifts the car, and they take a slower pace. "Sorry, this must be a busman's holiday for you. Didn't mean to talk God stuff. It's just that I feel I can talk to you, and you look so alluring listening to me." He lets his eyes rake over her.

"Eyes up here, buddy," Regina laughs. "And I never mind God talk. It's more than just a day job."

"Do people ever come to you with problems like mine?"

"All the time. Everyone is looking for God, even if they don't know it. And God is right there the whole time, even though they can't see Him."

"You think I'm imagining being alone?"

"I think you never looked to see who was behind you, lifting you up this whole time. That's God, but sometimes in the dark we can't see Him back there, and we get scared and feel forsaken."

"But I can't know God's there unless I see Him. There's no way to prove or disprove your argument."

"Yup, all you can go with is what you believe and what you've experienced. I'm asking you to consider having a different experience—one where you look for God instead of waiting for Him to pop out with jazz hands."

Roger laughs. "God with jazz hands! I wouldn't say I was waiting for that, but I take your point. Maybe I'll try it."

"Maybe? I thought a man like you reached out and grabbed what he wanted."

Roger pulls over to the side of the road and puts the car in park, turning on the hazard lights. He unbuckles his seatbelt and turns toward Regina. He brings up a hand to run a thumb along her jawline.

"Is this ok?" he asks in a low, quiet voice.

Regina can't quite think straight enough to speak, so she nods slowly. Roger brings his lips close to hers.

"Is this alright?"

As she nods, he brings his lips to claim hers for an all-consuming kiss. It almost stops Regina's heart. It's so good. Finally, he releases her, and they both sit, suddenly exhausted. Regina feels like she just ran a race and works on controlling her breath.

"So," she says, "that was…"

"Yeah," Roger finishes her thought. "I might not be able to let you go, Rev. Grant."

He turns on his signal and eases back into the light traffic. They ride in silence the rest of the way, each of them pondering how they haven't had a kiss like that since they were giddy teenagers.

Soon they are off the main roads and enter more residential areas. Palatial homes line the streets and more than a few gates keep out "undesirables." They come to a large iron gate with gold accents.

"I thought all the Hamptons was like a gated community? So you live in a gated community within a gated community."

"I'll answer if you promise not to make a face." Roger glances at her and finds her making a face to prove she is the contrary. "Oh well, this is Chez Moile."

Regina looks ahead to see the gates opening. They drive down a winding road and pass houses—they must be guest houses or something— any of which she would be happy to live in. But by now she is coming to understand she will forever be unprepared for Roger's world if she keeps comparing it to hers. The view opens up, and they come to a home so large it's probably a chore to get from one end to the other.

"So, this is your world."

"No, no," he quickly corrects, "this is just a house. I brought you here in hopes you can understand how I *feel* when I'm here—the freedom and camaraderie. That's what I want to share with you."

Regina dismisses her wonder at the scale of his

estate and focuses on what matters. "That sounds great. That was the whole reason I came to see Jonathan, to get away from it all."

"You can definitely do that here, although sometimes I still feel too connected. I'm plugged into the matrix. My phone, laptop, automatic gates, automatic lights, NFC door passes instead of keys—it's all too much. I promise, I really *am* a simple man."

"I know what you mean about being too plugged-in, a little anyway."

Regina sits quietly while Roger looks at her. She clears her throat, but he keeps staring.

"Well, I'd like to get out, but I have the feeling you're going to give me a talking to if I try to open my door, so..."

"I'm glad you're here. You're going to have a great time. I..."

"If I ever get out of the car," Regina laughs.

"Oh! Where are my manners? One moment."

Regina waits for him to get out and come around to her side to open her door when she is perfectly capable of doing it herself. But he is right. She *isn't* used to having someone there to help, so she tries it on for size.

"Thank you." Once again, she feels a little too close to him, only now she doesn't mind. "So, what are we going to do?" Her eyes grow wide like an eager kid's.

"What? Oh, let's get started by having me show you the grounds. My landscape team works very hard to make it delightful. You'll love it."

He takes her arm and drapes it over his as they begin their walk. Coming around the back of the main house, they enter a grassy plain with lush gardens on either side. In the flat area at the bottom of the back stairs are several people. Roger squeezes her hand and looks at her excitedly.

"Oh, good. You'll be able to meet the Captain before the party tonight!" He drags her towards the people.

It seems to Regina that there are two staff for every person at the party they are approaching. She tries to ignore the numbers and take in the scene. A middle-aged man and woman sit in ornate lawn chairs with enticing drinks in their hands.

An older man with a gnarled face holds a rifle—shotgun?—to his shoulder and yells, "Pull!"

A man releases a disc from some contraption Regina has never seen, and the older man shoots it into pieces in midair. She jumps involuntarily at the eruption of sound the gun makes.

"Get off my property, you salty, old man!" Roger claps an arm on the man, and they share a hug, and a punch or two in the shoulder.

"Roger, you bastard!" The man speaks in a gruff but friendly tone. "You're here early! You know the wife has the in-laws at my house with their 'sensitive ears' that can't tolerate a man enjoying himself. Driven out of my own house, by a woman!"

Regina was just noticing how charming he was until that last line. Roger turns to Regina with an arm around the man. They both wear broad smiles.

"Reverend Grant, may I introduce you to my good friend, Captain Seafood."

Regina cocks her head to the side, thrown by someone having a moniker like that. She puts out a hand and has the bejeesus shaken out of her arm. Stronger than he looks.

"Okay!" Regina reclaims her hand from the man's vigorous shaking. "*Captain Seafood*? How did that come to be?"

"What, are you from under a rock? I'm *the* Captain Seafood."

Regina looks at him with a pleasant but confused smile on her face.

"Geez, Roger, where are you finding your people these days?" He looks sternly at him, then turns to Regina and becomes a picture of gallantry. "Ma'am, I, Captain Seafood, CEO of CSea Restaurant Group, owner of *both* the Legor Seafood and McWallace and Chips fine seafood dining chains, am at your service." He bows exaggeratedly.

"A pleasure, Captain." Regina beams at him. Although he has said some things and behaved in ways she can't say she approves of, it's hard not to be sucked into his orbit by the pull of his charisma. "Is this skeet shooting, then?"

"Aw, Roger, where'd you get her? She's quaint!"

"I *try!*" Regina tries to be a good sport and hardly minds being called quaint.

"Linda, Garrett, meet..." he turns to her, "what did you say your name was again?"

"Regina."

"Ms? Mrs? Miss?"

She recognizes the greedy hunger in his eyes easily enough.

"*Reverend.*" Regina, perhaps wrongly, enjoys watching that sink in for him.

"Oh! Bless me, Father. I mean, Mother. Well, what the heck do I call you?"

"Regina. And stop asking about my status."

Captain Seafood looks offended. "You mistake me, good woman, for I am a married man. I was merely wondering what manner of lady good old Roger has brought into our midst." He leans down and kisses her hand.

"Charmed."

"Linda, Garrett, we gotta go!" He marches away with his long gun unloaded and hanging over his shoulder without saying goodbye or looking back.

Regina looks at Roger and laughs.

"I know, I know, he's a problem, but what can you do?"

"He's a force of nature." Regina has a hint of wonder in her voice.

The woman who had been sitting, Linda presumably, rushes by them. "Bye Roger, sorry, but see you at the party later." Regina's ears struggle to keep pace with the woman's fast cadence. "And nice to meet you, Rev. Grant. What are you dressing up as? Don't tell me—a nun?" She lets out an abrasive laugh. "Bye darlings!"

And with that, she is gone. The man who was seated approaches Regina and Roger with his hands in his slack pockets.

"Well, I'm not going to jump every time the Captain yanks the chain. I don't care if he *does* have more money than God. How are you, friend?" He claps a hand on Roger's back.

"Garret, it's good to see you. Allow me to introduce you to Rev. Regina Grant. Regina, meet Garrett Armins, Broadway producer and musician extraordinaire."

The tall, willowy man claims Regina's hand and brings it to his lips. "Charmed, I'm sure." Then he kisses her hand, only it's more like a slurp.

"Garrett, behave yourself. She's not a star struck actress waiting to fall into your arms." Roger's voice is a little hard.

Regina gets ready to comment that she is perfectly capable of telling Garrett that herself when she remembers what Roger said about accepting help. She closes her mouth and simply withdraws her hand.

"Oh, then why do you tempt me so? You never bring women here, and I'm just dying to know what's so special about this one. And a Reverend! Ooh, I *must* know if you can absolve me of my sins."

"I could, but I won't," Regina says flatly. She doesn't like him and instinctively edges away from him and towards Roger.

"Ooh, naughty minx."

She is about to make Garrett regret getting up that morning when Roger suddenly steps in front of her and between them.

"Did I stutter? I *said* behave." Roger's voice is iron.

Garrett looks soberly in his eyes for a moment, calculating, then is all smiles. "Ah, the artist's temperament. Sometimes I forget myself." He peers around Roger to Regina. "Do accept my apology, gracious lady. What is it they say—to err is human, to forgive is divine?"

Regina makes him wait several moments before she speaks. "Apology accepted."

Garrett gives her a look of delight, then looks at Roger. "There, you see, much ado about nothing. We're all friends here."

"Let's make sure we all *stay* friends," Roger answers.

"As you say. Well, I really must be off. See you at the party, where I will grace your ivories with my magic hands." He wiggles his fingers for emphasis. He retreats from them without breaking character.

Roger turns to face Regina and finds her standing with her arms crossed. He reads the annoyance in her eyes.

"If you're mad about me telling my friend to get in line instead of letting you do it, understand you are my guest here and your welfare is my responsibility... and I wanted to make sure you understand I don't approve."

She lets go of her annoyance because she knows she would have done the same, though she can't imagine any of her friends acting like Garrett did.

"Are these the friends you wanted me to meet?"

"We may be a bit of a motley crew, but they're my family. In my mind, it was all going to go fabulously. Sorry reality didn't live up to that."

"He seemed to think it was alright to act that way around you, I noticed." Regina doesn't mean for it to sound like an accusation and does her best to declare that with her softened tone.

Roger pauses a moment and, for the first time since she has met him, looks awkward. "I don't really bring women here, so it's never happened before."

"But I'm not a woman, I'm just someone you're helping with a potential job," Regina objects.

Roger steps back into her personal space and puts his hands on her arms. "You look very much like a woman to me." He draws out the words and lowers his mouth to hers.

Regina pulls her head back. "*What* is this party everyone is talking about, and why did Linda ask what I'm going as?"

Roger lifts his head and sighs at the lost moment. "Oh? Did I not mention the costume party tonight?" His smile is all mischief.

The Groove Line?

This night, Chez Moile is packed, and the party is jumping. It isn't like any party Regina has ever been to. There are so many VIPs, even *she* recognizes some of their names and faces. She peers out the window of the bedroom she has been assigned. Her room faces the front of the estate, and she sees car after car arrive to deposit people in lavish costumes before being whisked away by valets.

Regina sighs. It seems she had used up all of her extroversion eating her way across New York City the day before. She wants nothing more than to pet her cat and crawl into bed with a good book. But it's party time. She had asked to see his world, and here it is rushing to meet her.

She gathers her energy and propels herself out of her room. Walking down the curved staircase, she catches Roger, dressed as every bit of the swashbuckling sea pirate, staring at her. He pauses his conversation with someone and walks over to her.

"Rev. Grant, you look..." His eyes look her over as he searches for the right word.

"Don't say it. I already feel a little foolish dressed as the fairy godmother. It's a pretty fancy outfit."

Roger grabs her hand and places it on his arm. "You look beautiful, and I won't have you apologizing for it. Let me show you off to my friends."

Regina wants to say she isn't a curio piece to be displayed, but she swallows that misplaced complaint and embraces the moment.

"Here's somebody you know and love," Roger says, turning her to face the room, where she sees Jonathan and Ilana. They are dressed as Buster Brown and Little Bo Peep.

Regina rushes to hug them as if they have been apart for more than a few hours.

"It's so good to see you!" She steps back to take in Jonathan's costume. "Go on then," she says, twirling her finger to tell him to spin so she can admire the creation from every angle. He's dressed in a flowing hot pink blouse, pink—*were they called pantaloons when they ended tight at the calves?*—trousers with white socks, a black scarf around his neck for a tie, and a flat straw hat with a wide brim.

"*Why* are you dressed as Buster Brown? You look so ridiculous!" Regina laughs until she cries.

"Do you know how many Halloween parties I get invited to? And for each one you need a different costume. I read an old comic last week and got inspired. Don't tell me you don't like it? Ilana helped me put it together." Jonathan looks miffed his costuming ingenuity is not appreciated.

Regina looks at Ilana, wanting to know if she is even partially responsible for his outfit. She is all smiles. Aren't they a pair?

"I didn't say anything about you being dressed as a princess. A little old for that, don't you think?" Jonathan laughs.

Regina's eyebrows climb to the top of her head. "Are you *really* going to malign a woman's age? Besides, anyone can see," she shakes her wand in front of his face, "I'm the fairy godmother."

"Here to make all my dreams come true," Roger gushes.

His comment—the need in it—stops the conversation.

Regina looks at him for a moment, then takes her wand and bops him on the head with it. It breaks the tension.

"Jonathan, you'll never guess who I met shooting skeet," she looks to Roger, "is that it? Anyway, his name is *Captain Seafood*," she puts her best hardy fisher voice on, "and he's a most problematic old hoot!"

Jonathan cocks his head. "You met my boss?"

"Captain Seafood is your supervisor?"

"He's the *big* boss. Not that he even knows I'm alive or anything. I'm only mid-level in the company."

"My boy," Roger says, "He'll know you're alive tonight because he'll be here, and I will make it a point to introduce you." Roger glances at his watch. "He's no doubt aiming to be fashionably late."

"Don't tell me Captain Seafood is a diva?" Regina laughs.

"My *boss* is an accomplished titan of the restaurant industry. You've eaten at more of his restaurants than you realize." Jonathan defends.

Roger looks around to make sure no one's in earshot, then whispers, "And he's a bit of a diva."

They all laugh, even Jonathan. Regina wonders if he really thinks it's funny or if Roger is just the kind of man that you're obligated to laugh with when he makes a joke. She notices other guests coming to "kiss the ring" in acknowledging their host. She pushes thoughts she can't answer out of her way.

"You said you wanted me to meet your friends. How about we take a turn around the room and you make some introductions? I feel like granting more wishes!" She takes his offered arm, and they float over to a trio of people.

Jonathan stares after them. "He had better not be playing with Auntie."

Ilana pats his arm. "Roger Moile never *plays* at

anything."

Roger grazes his fingers across the knuckles of Regina's hand on his arm, and she reclaims her gloved hand. As he prepares to introduce Regina, Garrett sweeps into the great room and waves his black cape around with a flourish.

"Never fear, Garrett Armins is here," he shouts to no one in particular. "Here to entertain, amaze, and astound!" He takes the magician's hat from his head, produces a wand from an empty hand, taps the hat, and glitter explodes out of it. The partygoers ooh and ahh. Regina rolls her eyes.

Almost on cue, Captain Seafood arrives with an appropriately aged woman on his arm. Was Captain Seafood an old romantic or was she old money? He's dressed as Robin Hood, and she *might* be Friar Tuck. Regina can't tell.

They walk up to Roger and give a bow and curtesy before the Captain and Roger laugh.

"My good man, you outdo yourself every year, but I don't think I can identify your costume."

"Do you want me to tell you *which* pirate I am, or do you want to keep racking your brains for even the faintest clue?" Roger laughs, already knowing the answer.

"Oh, I'll get it before the night is over!" The Captain shakes a finger at him and then seems to notice Regina for the first time. "My good lady, you are a vision, indeed. Allow me to present my wife, Myrna."

"No," Regina protests, "she *has* to be a captain too, Captain!"

"Captain!" The Captain snorts and looks over his wife derisively, turning on a dime from the flowery introduction he had given only moments before. "Nah, this one's all dried up. Ah! The whiskey! You'll pardon me while I and your small batch single malt get better acquainted." He bows and walks off.

Regina looks at Myrna's glassy eyes and knows she's close to tears.

"I like your costume," Regina offers, still not sure who she's dressed as.

"Ooh," Myrna looks down at the brown wool cowl in frustration. "It's hot and uncomfortable. But thank you."

Regina is stunned silent for a moment at Myrna's exceptionally whiney voice. She hopes it is temporary.

"What made you and the Captain pick these outfits?"

"Oh! That's my honey. I do whatever he wants." She somehow sounded happy *and* whiney, to Regina's amazement.

"That's so... sweet."

"That's what marriage is—compromise. *Linda* would never understand that." Myrna says the name like she tastes something bitter. "That witch."

"Wrong costume, darling." Linda joins the group, clad head-to-toe in red with two horns sticking up from her spiky hair.

Myrna's face flushes, and she hurries away.

"Linda," Roger says in a tone of warning.

She shrugs. "If she wants to be married to the Captain she has *got* to toughen up, that's all there is to it."

Regina looks at Linda through veiled eyes, and Linda sees her looking.

"What, never seen a devil you couldn't exorcize before?"

"Never seen one so bold, to be honest."

"Life is wasted on the timid. Well, I'm going to mingle." She drifts away, looking for another way to be bold.

Regina turns and raises an eyebrow at Roger.

"*Your* friends."

Roger pinches the bridge of his nose. "Oh, this is going *great*."

Regina is drawn to help hurting people like a moth to a flame, so naturally she gravitates to Myrna, the Captain's wife. Only Myrna seems a bit too drunk to notice she is there, much less that Regina is trying to comfort her.

"I won't let her take him. I won't!" Her words are passionate but slurred.

"You and the Captain been married long?"

"Since he was a handsome ship's captain, when he was just Elford, not 'Captain Seafood.' Before all of this." Myrna's drink sloshes and spills as she gestures around the room.

"So you mean you don't come from money?" Regina assumes everyone here has always had money.

"Ha!" Myrna laughs. "We hardly had a pot to piss in starting out, just two kids from a small fishing town. But those days are far behind us now. The money changes everything. Linda doesn't want *him*," she scoffs. "She's not prepared for his night terrors, his demands, the realities of living with and loving an *old* man—those are all mine. The money changes everything."

"Do you regret it?"

Myrna stares into her empty martini glass for a few moments. "I hate it, but it's changed me—I can't live without it now... and he knows it."

"I'm really sorry. Is that why you're madder at Linda than you are the Captain?"

Myrna freezes midway in grabbing a drink from the tray of a passing waiter. "*Who* are you, again?"

"Nobody important."

"*Everybody* is someone important here, dear. Oh, that's right, you're Roger's *thing*. The Captain told me about you." She looks Regina up and down. It's clear she finds her wanting.

Regina does not shirk under her gaze and stays calm at being objectified. "I'm nobody's 'thing.'" She's also defensive because it's clear Myrna thinks she doesn't measure up. She takes a deep breath and starts over.

"It seems I got off on the wrong foot. I only meant to convey that it seems you're really unhappy, and I'm sorry."

Myrna tries to stare at her, but her eyes lose focus. Regina wonders if she's in this situation because she's a drunk, or if she's a drunk because she's in this situation.

"Yeah, well, watch it." She totters away unsteadily.

'Maybe she won't remember me when she wakes up,' Regina hopes.

Finding her way back to Roger, Regina is drawn to his pet parrot, the perfect accompaniment to his pirate costume. The large yellow and white bird sits perched on his shoulder, randomly shouting out phrases into the air.

"I hate to tell you, friend, but you're being upstaged," she says to Roger.

Holding up her hand to Roger's shoulder, the parrot he calls Bones perches on her hand, and she brings him closer to her. She pets his head and then under his arm, which Bones *really* likes.

"Aw, he likes me."

Roger and a few folks near him chuckle. "That 'affection' you're sensing may have more to do with the fact that a parrot's genitals are under its wings than anything else."

Regina's hand carefully pulls away from the bird, and she tries to place it back on Roger's shoulder, but now Bones can't seem to get enough of her and doesn't want to go. Those nearby laugh.

"So, *everybody* knows this charming piece of bird trivia but me?" Regina is only a little embarrassed that she felt up a pet and more incredulous that she is the only one who doesn't know where birds keep their family jewels.

Roger steps close to Regina. "Put your hand on my shoulder and leave it there for more than a millisecond. Bones will come home."

Once again, they are so close they're almost embracing, but the bird moves back onto his shoulder, and Regina wonders if she should wash her hands or not.

"Come with me," Roger says, then turns to the other guests. "Excuse us for just a moment."

He grabs her hand and walks her out of the room and towards the kitchens. Yes, *kitchens,* plural. They turn to the left at the end of a hallway and the walkway opens up to what seems to Regina to be three huge kitchens smashed together. No fewer than thirty people are hard at work, each playing their part in what looks like a well rehearsed routine.

"This is just *part* of what it takes to put this evening together. All the staff and event hires are paid well above the going rate, and it shows in the excellence of their products and service. It's a different world from yours, but I'm trying to do my best. I thought showing you I'm generous to the people who make this lifestyle possible might matter to you."

He turns away from the controlled chaos of the kitchen to face her. "It's been a long time since I've tried to impress someone like I'm trying to impress you. Is it working?"

"I'm making a note of it," she says coyly.

He grins. "Reverend Grant, are you *toying* with

me?"

She smiles mischievously, and his head lowers to hers. So close, she can hear his cell phone buzzing in his pocket.

"You gonna get that?" she whispers.

"In a minute." He closes the distance between their lips and kisses her.

A few of the workers in the kitchen hoot. Regina hardly notices.

The phone in his chest pocket continues to buzz between them. Finally, he withdraws his lips, and with a sigh, reaches for his phone.

"Hello," he says coolly, as if he hadn't just completely upended Regina's world.

"Has it been a whole minute?" she asks, wide-eyed to no one in particular.

Roger walks a few steps away from her to speak privately on the phone, and Regina tries to gather her wits. Roger is a *good* kisser, and it takes longer than she likes for her to clear her head and come back to the present. When he walks back to her, no longer on the phone, she can hardly remember her own name.

"Um, who was it?" she asks lamely.

"The woman who wants to interview you for the chaplain position. She wanted to meet you this evening, but I told her we're in Timbuktu until further notice." He gives a boyish grin.

Music from Garrett on the piano in the great room trickles into the kitchen area—is this actually an entire wing of the house?— reminding them there is a pretty great costume party going on.

"*You* are being a bad host."

Roger takes a breath in, telling her with his eyes that it's not host duties on his mind at the moment.

Still, he puts out his arm for her to take. "Shall we rejoin the party?" He glances at the bird on his shoulder. "What do you say, Bones?"

Bones squawks, "Party! Party!"

They head over to the piano where Garrett plays Broadway hits. It's fun, and, though Regina's not much of a theater-goer, she recognizes some tunes and sings along to the choruses. She is floating on clouds from the kiss and barely has space to remember Garrett is vile.

Is that how the rest of them do it? Just fill their lives with so many pretty, fancy things that they don't even notice the ugliness so close at hand? She knows he's Roger's friend, but she resolves to knee him in the groin if he attempts to slurp on her hand again. Some people only respect and respond to violence, she laments.

Friends, How Many of Us Have Them?

The room erupts with applause after Garrett finishes a song with a flourish.

"Thank you, thank you. Just one of the many numbers you will hear exclusively at my upcoming musical. Broadway hasn't heard the last from me!" Garrett's swagger oozes from the words and there is a small round of applause.

"Garrett, this is great! I knew you hadn't produced anything in a while and just assumed you were on some top secret project. Is this what you've been working on behind the scenes?" someone asks.

Garrett's smile is meant to convey an affirmative answer, but Regina can see from the way it doesn't reach his eyes that it's not exactly the truth. Perhaps she's over eager to see faults in him, but see them she does.

"Oh, has it been a while?" she inquires. "Why the lapse?"

"Didn't you hear the man?" Roger answers, "It's all been part of his master plan."

"I *am* listening, and he didn't actually say that, so I was just curious." Regina smiles sweetly and tries to maintain a light tone.

The veil over Garrett's eyes wavers for a bit, then he throws up his hands.

"My dear Roger, how dare you bring this truth

teller into our midsts! It's as you say, ma'am, I *have* been away, through no fault of my own. I faced baseless charges, though it took *quite* a bit of money to make them go away. But now that I have handled the matter, Broadway has welcomed me back with open arms, and there was much rejoicing in the land!" Garrett smiles reassuringly to the people listening.

Those who have hung around for the story applaud. Roger cocks his head.

"You told me they dropped the charges. You *settled*?"

"It *is* the way of the world these days, even for *innocent* men." Garrett places a hand over his heart and looks absolutely angelic for a moment.

"Mmm," Roger frowns.

Regina sees him in thought and is glad he may be reckoning with the fact that Garrett is far from harmless.

"Hey, Auntie. Where you been?" Jonathan and Elena pop up beside her.

"Nowhere," she says coolly, but her cheeks redden at memories of her kitchen kiss.

Loud voices capture the attention of the room.

"You are to shut up and do as you're told!" Captain Seafood's gruff voice is still lovable, even when he's talking down to a grown woman.

"But I wanna go home!" Myrna whines loudly. Her voice seems pitched to trigger the same reaction as nails down a chalkboard for Regina.

"You are impossible. Fine, woman, let's go!" He cuts a path through the great room, placing a hand on Roger's arm as he passes, looking surly and thwarted.

The only one in the room whose eyes don't seem glued to Captain Seafood is Linda, who knocks back a martini and seems very interested in her glass as the room watches the scene play out. Many turn their gaze on her—the *open* secret.

"What?!" Linda shouts as she looks around the room, daring anyone to call her Captain Seafood's mistress. She slams her glass down so hard it breaks and cuts her hand.

"Oh, no," Regina rushes forward. "Let's get your wound cleaned and bandaged."

"I'm fine." Linda snatches away her bleeding hand.

"Please don't bleed all over this nice rug by being strong and defiant." Regina glances at Roger. "I've learned that's not *always* the best way. Let's go to the kitchen and get a first aid kit. Luckily, you're already wearing red, so no wardrobe change required, haha," Regina laughs lamely. "And we probably got off on the wrong foot. I'd like to help." She looks at Linda with hopeful eyes.

Regina doesn't give her a chance to answer, simply dragging her to the kitchens like a reluctant toddler. There she gets help from the staff in locating a first aid kit and cleans and dresses the wound.

"Why are you like this?" Linda, who has stayed silent until now, asks.

"Like what?" Regina places tape over the gauze.

"You don't owe me anything, so you must want something," Linda says decisively.

"I like to think I'm a nice person, but I also feel bad about not making the best impression. I don't understand everything that's going on with you, the Captain, and Myrna, but it's none of my business. I'm just trying to get to know you as Roger's friend."

Linda gives her an assessing look. "We'll see." She inspects the job Regina has done on her hand. "Well... thank you." She almost chokes getting the words out.

"My pleasure," she beams. "Care to shake a tail

feather?"

Linda's laugh surprises her. "You might just be alright, preacher."

Regina knows she's playing with fire with someone like Linda, but she always gives people the benefit of the doubt.

It's going to get her killed one day.

Afoot!

Jonathan and Ilana take in the crisp evening air near the front of the estate.

"I wish I could give you all this," Jonathan declares.

"You *know* I don't need it, but I'm not saying I would mind it either!"

They laugh together.

"Did you really mean what you and Regina said? I had no idea you were so suspicious of wealth! I can tell you now I plan to be obscenely rich. Will you still love me?"

"Of course, all the way to the bank, baby! You know I..." His voice trails off as he notices a strange movement of light from a window on the second floor. Ilana turns and follows his gaze. It looks like a flashlight slashing through the dark. "Is *that* the room Roger assigned to us?"

"Yes," Ilana says grimly. She leans into Jonathan's side in fear, but he is already moving forward. "Where are you going?"

Jonathan, often boyish and bookish, is all bravery and tactics now.

"That room is our home, at least for the night. I'm not letting someone ransack our home. Go find Roger and tell him. I'll deal with our little cat burglar."

Ilana lets him be brave and finds Roger, telling him and Regina about the strange sight and Jonathan's mission to catch the intruder. Roger makes eye contact with a man that has been standing quietly on the wall of the great room. Regina hadn't noticed him before, but as he steps forward, she can see the bearing of military training. His steps are all the same length and he takes in everything about his surroundings as he closes the distance to Roger. Of course, he has a bodyguard, Regina thinks, surprised she hasn't thought of it before. Roger and the man share a few quiet words before the man retreats with a single point of focus that even shows up in how he leaves the room.

"Ilana, don't worry, I have my man on it now. Let's go to my office and meet our interloper. My man will meet us there with him and Jonathan in tow."

In Roger's office, Regina meets another side of the man but is too distracted worrying about Jonathan to fully appreciate it. Whereas the art was massive and abstract in his corporate office, this room almost looks like a storage space of old knick knacks, haphazardly placed. Is this his office or his trophy room?

A baseball glove rests on stacks of baseball cards. A tacky Katana sword is mounted on the wall. Probably the real thing, she corrects herself. Maybe made by a blade master at the top of a mountain that only forges once a year, or something similarly rare and impossible to get. So, perhaps not tacky.

Why he would choose to bring a potential enemy—what else could a burglar be—into a place that reveals so much of himself? Regina can't understand.

Jonathan walks in the door to join them. He appears unhurt, and both Regina and Ilana jump up from their seats in relief. Regina lets the two lovers reunite after the threat of violence and settles for catching his eye and letting the relief on her face show she was worried and is glad he's safe.

Roger's "man" enters behind Jonathan, escorting a flawlessly dressed man in a fitted tuxedo. As Regina is coming to understand, a perfect fit usually means it's custom. It seems this is no ordinary burglar.

"And what makes you think you can disturb the inviolate peace of my home?" Regina hears the anger in Roger's voice.

"My good man, I am simply doing my job," the burglar says in an English accent. He reaches—slowly, when he sees Roger's man reaching for the gun on his shoulder holster—into his inside jacket pocket and produces a card. He tries to hand the card to Roger but his man intercepts and inspects it first, then hands it to Roger.

Roger turns hard eyes on the man. "Why is a so-called 'private detective' in my house? Archibald Mansfield," he says, reading the name on the card, "why should I not call the police and have you arrested?"

"Oh, but you *should*... unless you want to keep any of your friends, that is. If you call the police, it would force me to tell them what I do. Then suspicion falls on every one of your guests as they try to distance themselves from you and the horse you rode in on." The man laughs incredulously, knowing he's untouchable.

"What are you doing here?" Roger asks.

Archibald thinks for a moment, then answers. "I'm investigating on behalf of my client on a matter of business subterfuge and corporate espionage."

"Who is your client?"

"Someone at this party. That is all I will say."

"Why were you in my home?"

"Investigating, dear man."

"Am I to surmise by your presence with a flashlight under the cover of darkness in my guest bedrooms that the agent of this subterfuge you're investigating is *also* a guest at my party?"

"That is yet to be determined. Investigation takes me to the most interesting places. This party, for example! So many people dressed up just for sport.

Capital idea." He turns to Regina. "My pleasure, Fairy Godmother." He gives her a pleasant nod and turns to Jonathan. "Ah yes, the source of my apprehension. I didn't know young people even knew who Buster Brown *was*. Well done." He gives another nod. "My lady," he speaks to Ilana, "the most charming Little Bo Peep I have ever seen!" His eyes sparkle, as if he's not at all restrained or bothered by any part of his evening.

"*You*," as he turns to Roger's man, "are aptly dressed as a common thug," he says dismissively.

Archibald turns his gaze back to Roger. "But you, I can't figure out. You can't just be *any* pirate, that's too easy. I do love a challenge! Care to give me any hints?"

"No, Mr. Mansfield, I do not. I would like you off my property. Now."

"Ah well, it seems like such a lovely party, but I must be off." Archibald clasps his hands together and speaks as if leaving is all his idea.

On his way out of the room, his eyes linger on a picture of a group of apartment buildings. He turns suddenly, and Roger's man steps towards him.

"You're dressed as Black Caesar! I knew I would get it! I can't leave loose ends. Call it a personal failing that makes me good at my profession. I can uncover *any* secret, even your charming disguise, sir."

Roger's eyes turn to his man, who takes hold of Archibald's arm.

"Unhand me, my good man! I need no escort."

"But you will have one. See this man off my grounds, please."

Archibald collects himself, smiles at the ladies, then gives Roger's man a stern look. "Let's have an understanding, you and I. Touch me again and you will be profoundly sorry. Well, I am off, gentle people. Enjoy the rest of your festivities." He walks out of the room as if he owns Chez Moile—lock, stock, and barrel.

"Even your burglars are classy," Regina says with wonder.

Roger stares at the man's card, then places it on his desk and turns his attention to the people in the room.

"Ilana, Jonathan, Rev. Grant, I hope you will keep this unfortunate matter in the strictest of confidence. Mr. Mansfield is right. Revealing his presence here could provide headaches for my guests."

Jonathan and Ilana voice their complete cooperation, but Regina does not. Roger turns to Regina and cocks his head, trying to figure her out.

"You're not lying, you're just omitting, if that's what you're wondering," he offers.

"If someone asks me, I *will* tell them, but I won't volunteer the information. Good enough?"

"Good enough," he nods. He continues looking at her, "Are you really as good a person as you seem *all* the time?"

"Ha!" Jonathan erupts. "She was the best liar of all of us growing up. Don't let the collar fool you!"

Regina turns a stern look on Jonathan. "I have no idea what you mean," she says in a lofty, impervious tone.

"That's something I *definitely* have to hear more about, but for right now, I think it's time to take this party to the next level. 'Electric Slide,' anyone?"

"Now you're talking," Regina exclaims. "Let's get our dance fever on!"

They pile out of his office and head back to the party. On their way, Regina pulls Jonathan to the side.

"Are you going to tell me *this* is normal, too?"

Jonathan shakes his head and lets out the breath. "We're through the looking glass now, Auntie."

Murder Most Foul

After discovering the dead body...

Everyone who has stayed overnight at Chez Moile, presumably having partied too hard to go home, is gathered in the great room like reluctant children. Regina imagines people like them are not used to being told they can't do whatever they want. So, it stings when local law enforcement prevents them from leaving the premises.

But the cops have said they are not to leave the *property*, not stay stuck in the main house. Regina smiles as she sits on one of the benches outside, looking into the great room. She likes to get her tiny declarations of freedom and independence out when she can.

She can see Detective Simms in the great room, pacing in front of the guests as he asks questions and scribbles in a notepad. He reminds her of Columbo. She hopes and prays he knows what he's doing.

"So, you are telling me *no one* heard a shot in the middle of the night?" Detective Simms flips through his notepad, reminding himself of the individual interviews with guests he has conducted. He nods his head absentmindedly as he paces.

The room's frustrations seem to bubble over and groans erupt from people as they shift in their seating.

"I'm wondering how many times you're going to ask us that," Linda says from the chaise lounge she's draped over. "We have already told you, no one heard anything. It was a *party,* and the music was loud late into the night." She stands and stalks toward the man. "Captain Seafood is dead, and you seem to have no sense of urgency. I'm thinking this is beyond you, detective. *One* detective for the Captain? This is a joke."

She crosses her arms and continues to stare him down, standing over him at her graceful height. To his credit, he barely seems to notice her powerful displeasure.

"Ma'am, just what exactly is your relationship with the deceased?"

"I worked with him. *What* are you even writing in your notebook? I've already told you this."

"Is that the *whole* of your relationship with the Captain?" Simms looks up from his notepad and takes Linda in.

"That's all *you* need to know, little man." She steps closer to him.

"Well, with all due respect, *everyone* is little compared to you." He lets out a small chuckle and writes something in his notepad.

Linda scoffs and walks off. The detective looks, a little longingly, after her for a moment before turning his attention back to the room.

"Who here was the last person to see the victim?" The detective stands with his notepad ready.

The room discusses who had seen him when. Regina doesn't know why that is necessary. Everyone had seen him leave in a huff when his wife requested. It was quite the spectacle. It made no sense. Were they covering for Myrna?

The screech of car brakes outside grabs the room's attention. If Regina can believe her ears, that high-pitched shrieking belongs to Myrna. Her heart aches for the Captain's wife—now his widow. She must have driven here in her grief to see the body.

Regina realizes she's heading towards her without deciding to do it. She sees two police officers trying to block her way into the house. Myrna is a holy terror. Obviously drunk, she yells for the cops to leave her alone while she sways dangerously.

Regina rushes forward to get between Myrna and the cop, who, in her opinion, is being rough for no reason.

"Whoa, whoa, whoa. We're good here. I've got her," she assures the cops. "Myrna, you want to come inside?"

Regina speaks in an easy tone and with confidence, but has no idea what she's going to do with Myrna. She's like a caged tiger, ready to make a break for it.

"He's dead!" She shrieks as she almost stumbles to the ground. Regina hopes Myrna didn't kill anyone on her drunken drive over here.

She sees two other officers join the scene and ring Myrna and realizes if she doesn't restrain Myrna, they will. She throws her arms around Myrna in a bear hug.

"I'm so sorry. Let me mourn with you," Regina whispers in her ear. She almost falls down in the next moment when Myrna goes as limp as a rag doll in her arms. Her sobs turn soft. Grief is violent and abrupt.

A long, sleek car pulls up to them... and out from the back steps Captain Seafood!

"What in tarnation is going on here? What are all these cops for? Myrna, what have you gotten yourself into?"

Myrna screams in a pitch so disturbing that it makes Regina's ears pop. She comes back to life and wrestles out of Regina's hold and literally hurls herself into the Captain's arms.

"But you're dead!" she cries as she kisses his face.

By now the others inside have come out to stare, mouths agape, at Captain Seafood and his wife, Myrna, nearly plastered onto him.

The Captain looks at Roger, "Good God, man, you *have* to tell me what's going on!"

Roger almost runs the short distance to him, then claps a hand on his shoulder, as if to confirm he is real. "Captain, we thought you were dead!"

"Dead?! I'm as immortal as they come!"

Regina walks over to the detective. "So, who was the dead man in the Robin Hood costume, and did the killer mean to kill *him* or the Captain?"

The Nitty Gritty

By the afternoon, patience at being told they can't leave the property is wearing thin on everyone. Most have gone off to separate wings of the house to conduct their affairs in peace.

"Everyone in the...," she hears paper rustling, "...all at *Chez Moile*, gather in the great room for questioning." The voice blares out from an intercom on the wall by her bedroom door.

It's Regina's first time seeing all of Roger's staff gathered. She is not shocked but still has a hard time conceptualizing that there was one staff member for every guest. They gather, most in their uniforms, off to one side of the great room, but Roger still mingles with them, shaking hands and talking to them as if he invited them to the party.

Detective Simms enters the room, head in his small notebook. Finally, he looks up. "Who is Archibald Mansfield? Raise your hand if you know him."

Regina looks at Roger's man, standing near the grand piano with the other staff, but sees him staring blankly ahead. She looks at Roger and raises a questioning eyebrow. Is he really not going to say anything? She stands up, puts her hands on her hips, and puts the full weight of her displeasure into her stare. Finally, Roger, then his man, then Regina raise their hands.

"Was that so hard?" Regina almost rolls her eyes in annoyance, but she had known it might come to this when Roger asked them to keep the matter to themselves last night.

"Mr. Moile, would you care to enlighten us?" The detective turns to a fresh page in his notebook.

Regina makes her way back outside as Roger explains the break-in last night and how he came to know Archibald Mansfield, private detective. The detective questions him more closely.

"Who would want to kill someone who wasn't even supposed to be here?" Detective Simms asks.

"Perhaps I can shed some light on that," Captain Seafood offers. "Archibald Mansfield was in my employ. Let's just say I was having some business troubles. Subterfuge! Every location for the last two years that I have wanted for restaurant expansion has been bought out from under me at the last possible moment. It's cost me millions!

"I hired Archibald to get to the bottom of it. He called me yesterday saying he had indeed found signs of malfeasance. He said he would meet me here to reveal all. That's why I was so upset the wife made me leave early."

"I'm not happy that my home was made the location of this secret rendezvous, but no one asked me." Roger crosses his arms in displeasure. "Why *here*?"

The Captain shrugs. "I guess he thought it would be somebody at the party. Now I'll never know."

Detective Simms flips to a fresh page in his notebook and keeps scribbling. "Sounds like whoever was cheating you had a lot of motivation to stay undiscovered."

The detective looks outside but can't figure out what caught his eye and returns to his notebook. "I need to know...," he stares again through the open door.

He sees Regina climbing the lattice on the wall of the house.

"Is your lady trying to break into your home *in front* of us?" Detective Simms sounds truly dumbfounded.

"She's not his lady," Jonathan pipes up, then looks bashful as everyone in the room looks at him questioningly. "They just met two days ago," he explains shyly.

Walking outside, Detective Simms waits for her to descend the lattice onto the ground.

"Usually cat burglars wait until it's night, and make sure there are not a ton of cops around." Simms taps his notebook against his head to indicate the woman should use her head more.

"Exactly," Regina responds as she checks her hands for splinters after having climbed up and back down the lattice on the outer wall of the house.

"Ma'am?" The detective is confused.

"Poor Mr. Mansfield was essentially a cat burglar last night. He would have been much better than I."

"Agreed," Simms added, a little too readily, in Regina's eyes, and she reminds herself he is right.

"He would never have worn hard-soled shoes," Regina says definitively.

"What's that got to do with anything?"

"He couldn't have climbed the trellis to get into the bedrooms on the second floor with hard-soled shoes. I barely made it in my sneakers just now."

"Oookay," Simms says, not quite following.

"The body in the pool that we now know is Archibald and *not* Captain Seafood was wearing hard-soled shoes. Even if he was dressing as the Captain, he would not have worn shoes he couldn't climb in. That means he didn't put those shoes on himself."

"If he didn't put the *shoes* on himself..."

"Then what are the odds that he didn't put on the costume himself, either?" Regina asks, finishing the detective's sentence. "Someone wanted us to *think* they were trying to kill the Captain but had a case of mistaken identity. Archibald Mansfield was the target all along."

The Not Quite Midnight Train

"Rev. Grant, I really wish we could part under different circumstances." Roger holds her gaze as Jonathan and Ilana wait for her in their car.

"Vacation's over. Plus, murder and all. But thank you for being such a gracious host."

Roger steps closer to her. "Is that all I am, a host, to you?"

"I *said* gracious," Regina draws out playfully. "I'll call you before I leave the city."

She unlocks her phone, creates a new contact and hands it to him to fill in his information.

"Please let me take you to dinner tonight. I should only be a few hours behind you in heading back." Roger taps his details into her phone and hands it back to her.

"I really want to spend some time with Jonathan and Ilana, if that's alright." Regina tries to be demure. She can't imagine many people say no to him.

"I see. Well, I'll fly to DC to see you next week."

"I hope they find out who killed poor Archibald by then."

Roger cocks his head. "*Poor* Archibald? I'm sorry that he's dead, but it's part of the risk of being a private investigator. I'm not sure he deserves your pity."

"He was alive, and now he is no more because someone else decided it was time for him to die. I'll give him pity and *more* if I want."

Roger raises his hands in surrender. "Didn't mean to wake the compassionate beast. I give up," he jokes.

Regina is in the mood to let it go. She leans in to give him a hug but turns her face so that his lips land on her cheek instead of her mouth.

"Bye Roger."

He pulls her back to him, intending to kiss her as a car horn sounds. Turning, they look at Jonathan in the car with an impish grin. "Time to get a move on," he says.

Regina hops in the backseat and they are off. When they reach the gates exiting the property, Detective Simms flags them down and invites himself into the back seat with Regina without bothering to say hello. He flips through his notebook until he finds the page he wants.

"Regina Grant. *Reverend* Regina Grant. Pretty good head you got on your shoulders."

"Thanks."

"Listen, you seem like some more normal folks that I can relate to. Nothing close to murder ever happens in this district. I'll admit, I'm in a little over my head. Would you mind if I bounced some things off you, Rev. Grant? Like a sounding board." He taps his pen a-rhythmically against the notebook.

"Detective Simms, I'm truly flattered, but I'm no investigator. I'm sure you've got everything well in hand. Besides, I'm leaving."

Detective Simms puts his notebook and pen away. "Too bad, ma'am, but thanks for the vote of confidence."

He gets out of the car and walks away without shutting the door. Maybe he *doesn't* have this well in hand, Regina worries. Leaning over, she shuts the door, and they exit Chez Moile.

"I'm not gonna call him daddy," Jonathan teases and bursts with laughter.

"Ha. Ha," Regina answers flatly.

Ilana taps Jonathan for him to be quiet when she sees the sober look on Regina's face. "Everything alright?" she asks.

Jonathan eyes her in the rear-view mirror and stops joking. "What's wrong? Is this because he's a billionaire?"

"With a 'B?'" Regina asks, stunned, before she clears her head. "No, it's not because he's wealthy. It's just that he's wrong about his feelings for me."

"What does *that* mean? From what I saw, he seems pretty clear about what he wants." Jonathan smirks.

"This is grown folks' business, nephew," she says with the best old lady voice she can muster.

"If you don't stop, I am *three* years younger than you, Auntie."

"Only answer you're gonna get out of me, young man," Regina laughs, sits back, and closes her eyes to indicate the matter is done.

Behind her eyelids, she searches for a way to get out of her predicament. It is easy to stop thinking about Roger and think about poor Archibald's murder. It *had* to be whoever he was going to reveal that night to the Captain. Didn't it?

But why would they go through the farce of dressing him as Captain Seafood? Surely, they had to know that couldn't fool anyone for long. There are too many pieces of the puzzle missing for her to hazard any guesses, but it seems like she had been at a costume party with a murderer.

The next morning, Regina is back in her hotel—now that she has stayed in a mansion, how unacceptable things seem here—packing for her train home. She looks at her phone and sees multiple missed call notifications from Roger, which she dismisses. She put her phone on do not disturb yesterday and hasn't taken it off yet. It gives her an excuse not to answer Roger's calls.

Ordering a rideshare from her phone, she's glad she insisted Jonathan and Ilana go into work as scheduled and leave her to make her own way to the train station. They had more than enough excitement during her visit, and she wants them to get back to normal.

After nearly losing her life—at least it feels that way—Regina staggers from the taxi and into the station. The driver had sped like a madman through packed streets, where no one seemed to care about traffic laws. She is feeling the pinch of New York City and is glad to be returning to her home, if not her situation.

She tries hard not to look too bewildered inside as she looks for her train's track number and heads there. 'Don't look at anybody. It's not your business. Keep your bags close to you. Walk fast—if you're slow, you're just asking for it,' she tells herself. She's so focused on ignoring people, she almost misses someone calling her name.

"Ilana?"

Ilana runs up to her, then takes a moment to catch her breath. "Thank God I caught you. You're not answering your phone!"

"What's wrong? Where's Jonathan?" Regina doesn't like the alarm in Ilana's voice.

"He's at the police station. They've arrested him for the murder of Archibald Mansfield!"

Rally!

Regina isn't catholic, but she gets out her rosary beads and rubs them between her fingers to focus her mind and keep her calm.

"Bail," she breaks the silence in the taxi on the way to the precinct holding Jonathan. "When will we be able to get him out? How much will it *cost*? I can start calling family to get something together."

"No need. Roger's on it." Ilana wrings her hands.

"Roger?"

"I burst into his office as soon as I heard. I figured, it all happened on his estate, he should care about what happens to his guests. And I was hoping he would care about Jonathan for your sake. Looks like I was right."

They pull up to the police station in time to see Roger and Jonathan descending the steps. Regina hangs back, knowing it's best not to separate young lovers at times like these. She doesn't hug him any less fiercely for being second, though.

"Why don't we get out of the street?" Roger suggests. "There's a diner across the street. What do you say we hold an impromptu war council and strategize?"

Regina sees Detective Simms at the doors to the station. "You all go ahead, I'll catch up to you." Roger follows her eyes to the detective and nods as he guides Jonathan and Ilana to the diner. Regina hurries up the stairs while she can still see the detective. He sees her, makes a quizzical face, then flips through his notebook.

"Oh," he says in understanding, "He's your nephew. I'm sorry about Jonathan's arrest."

"*What* is going on? He's no killer. Why do they even suspect him? Is this how you handle your investigation? I wish I had..."

"Whoa, whoa, whoa. Just hold on a minute." Detective Simms pulls her to the side away from the main doors and continues. "This is no longer my investigation. I told you we don't get murders in my jurisdiction and there were a lot of important people involved. It's out of my hands now.

"But I've got to tell you, the case against your nephew seems pretty open and shut. He worked for the Captain and had access to sensitive information. A second search of the bedroom he and..." he flips through his notebook again, "...Ilana had revealed the very documents the Captain thought were being stolen. Jonathan confronted Archibald Mansfield in the act of trying to uncover him. Later, he finished the job and dressed him as the Captain to cover his tracks and create confusion."

Regina feels dazed for a moment as he lays out the case against Jonathan. She can't believe this is happening. Her head cocks to the side.

"A *second* search? Why was nothing found on the first search? Between the murder and the time of this second search, anybody could have put these incriminating documents there. It doesn't seem very open and shut to me!" Regina forces herself to take deep breaths to calm down.

Simms looks around him to make sure no one is nearby. "They want it that way. All the East Hamptons is on edge. If the wealthy can't be safe in their gated communities, that's a problem that has to be solved. Your Jonathan is not one of them. It needs to be him." He looks regretfully at her as if the judgment on

Jonathan has already been handed down.

"If I tell you I *know* my nephew, Jonathan, did not kill anyone, do you believe me?"

He gives her an assessing look. "I believe *you* believe it. More than that, I'll need evidence."

"What do you say we find some? I *know* you can't like the way this is going down." Regina prays his offer from earlier still stands.

The detective scrawls his phone number on a piece of paper and tears it from his notebook. "So long as you understand that my main purpose can't be to exonerate Jonathan. I'm after the real killer."

"*Thank you*," she gushes as she takes the paper greedily from his outstretched hand.

"I get the feeling you're not exactly cop-friendly. I want you to know there's a lot of us good guys out there, despite all this madness your nephew's caught up in."

"*Now* who's detective-ing?" Regina smiles. "What gave me away?"

"I saw the way you positioned yourself between the Captain's wife and the cops. You thought they were going to hurt her. You were *wrong* about that by the way—I run a tight ship—but I admire your defense of those who are in a tough spot. This whole thing needs a shrewder eye than I have. Maybe together we can make some progress. Deal?"

Regina puts out her hand and shakes the detective's heartily. "Deal."

Fifteen minutes later, she is across the street in the diner with Roger, Jonathan, and Ilana. They all have coffee except for Regina, who orders hot water and fishes a ginkgo biloba tea bag from her purse. She needs all the brain power she can get right now. As she waits for her tea to steep, she looks across the street at the police precinct.

"I'm so sorry they locked you up in there. I *know* it wasn't nothing." Regina reaches out and grabs Jonathan's hand.

Jonathan's "everything is fine" mask slips for a moment and she sees the fear and pain in his eyes.

"I won't let you go back, I promise you." Regina knows there are no guarantees in life like the one she makes now, but she will bend heaven and earth to be the exception.

Roger speaks up at the table. "Rev. Grant, I promise you nothing will happen to him. I have my lawyers on the case, and they will make the attorney general's office rue the day they went forward with this case. Jonathan, you'll be fine."

Regina is only half listening as she watches Linda—the Captain's "open secret" descend the steps of the police station.

"Gotta go." She flies from the table and hurries across the street to intercept her.

Out of breath—she needs to exercise more—she catches up to Linda hailing a cab.

"Miss Linda, hi! I know you're as glad as we are that the Captain is alive." She stops and takes a few deep breaths. "I don't know if you heard, but the police have arrested my nephew, Jonathan, for the murder of Archibald Mansfield. We just got him out and we're over in the cafe planning if you want to join us."

"Yes, that's unfortunate. I have somewhere else to be, so I won't be joining you."

"Roger's with us." Regina pulls out proximity to power to tempt her and sees her waver for a minute. "I would think you would want to shore up your position in this matter as well. Some might say *you* had motivation to kill the Captain as his mistress or to kill Archibald as a threat to the company you work for. We can all coordinate our strategies."

Linda lets out a loud laugh that seems out of place on the streets, but of course all the passers-by just mind their own business.

"I'm sorry about Jonathan. He's a good worker, but all of this has nothing to do with me. I've just been officially cleared. I have the perfect alibi. You may want to cover your ears, but the Captain and I were together when the murder happened. I couldn't have killed that man, so this no longer concerns me."

Regina searches for a way to get her on board. "Could I just *ask* you, then? Will you help us?"

Linda looks at her appraisingly. "This is nothing personal, but don't think we're friends just because you put a bandage on me once. You've got Roger's help. Nice job with that, as one kept woman to another. You don't need me. And, I don't want to. But I'm sure our paths will cross again as you continue to insinuate your way into Roger's life. I'll be sure to keep it friendly, and I expect you to do the same. Goodbye."

She opens the door to a waiting cab and rides away. Regina walks, dazed, back to the cafe, simply allowing herself to be carried along by the crowd of people. Sitting back down at the cafe table, she marshals her focus back to the task at hand.

"So this whole thing is about corporate espionage they're thinking? Who better to be the *true* culprit than the Captain's right-hand woman? How much do you *really* know about Linda?"

"Wait a minute, Linda's my friend," Roger protests.

"Somebody at that party killed poor Archibald. We have to start clearing names off the board until we find who did it. If she's got nothing to hide, then we'll clear her."

"And how do you intend to determine that?"

"Jonathan, don't you and Linda work in the same office?"

"Yes," he says reluctantly, not liking where he thinks his aunt is going.

"Perfect. Let's just go after hours tonight and have a look at her files to see if she's the one that's been leaking information to the Captain's competition."

"She's my *boss*. Are you trying to get me fired?"

"I'm trying to keep you out of jail and exonerate your name! You had better have the same agenda or this could go a whole different way. I'm your family and I can't let anything happen to you. Besides, it's not even breaking and entering since you work there. It's just a little investigating."

Jonathan looks at Ilana. "Do you see what I'm dealing with here?"

"I'm with her on this one. This isn't something that's going to clear up on its own. We have to fight for your freedom every way we know how. I *know* the prison system isn't kind to Black men, and I won't let that happen to you. *Nothing* is off the table." Ilana speaks fiercely, and they all see the tears in her eyes.

Jonathan hugs her. "I'm not going anywhere. I'm taking this seriously and will do what I have to do." He draws himself up and exudes the strength Regina knows he will need to get through this. "So, when are we doing this?"

"Tonight, obviously."

Jonathan grimaces. "Tonight, then... You're playing the *Mission Impossible* theme in your head right now."

"Guilty!" Regina chirps excitedly. She wonders if she has time to score an all-black outfit to look the part. Tonight, she's going to explore all of Linda's secrets.

The Crosstown Express

Jonathan looks up at the skyscraper that houses Captain Seafood's CSea Restaurant Group. "I can't believe we're going to do this."

Regina pulls him toward the building. "Come on, before you lose your nerve."

They walk by a security desk inside where Jonathan waves at the guards before swiping his access card to pass through the gates to the elevators. Regina stays close and steps through the briefly opening gates with him. When they are in the elevator on their way to the 23rd floor, Jonathan lets out a breath.

"Calm down. No breaking and entering, just entering. You have every right to be here." She speaks in calm, even tones, hoping to relax him. She hates to see him this stressed, but she knows they have to fight with all they are to save him, and she needs his help.

"So, the Captain said someone has been buying out the locations for his future restaurants out from under him, right? Can you dig up all the information on his last few locations? We need to do the same things that Archibald was doing to find the spy. It had to be someone who worked here to be able to plant evidence in your room at Chez Moile. My money's on Linda."

"Why would she work against the Captain? They're together."

"You *can't* be that naïve! Linda loves power, the Captain—only so much as he can give it to her. If crossing him gives her the greater benefit, she will turn on him in a heartbeat, I just know it."

"You're judging her pretty harshly."

"You're her employee. Your arrest is bad for the company. Even if she doesn't want to stand up for you personally, why won't she at least protect her company from bad publicity? She is choosing not to help you, and I want to know why."

"Never looked at it that way." Jonathan lets the facts sink in. "What's the plan?"

"We've got to think like Archibald Mansfield and follow the evidence. You pull the information about the Captain's last few location acquisitions that went awry. I'll look in Linda's office for... something."

"Ok." Jonathan heads in one direction.

"Wait, where is Linda's office?" Regina asks bashfully.

"What?! I thought you were playing the crack investigator. Shouldn't you already know, Auntie?"

"Are you taking this seriously?"

Jonathan lets down his jovial mask. "I know I'm fighting for my life. This is how I'm keeping my cool about it."

"Well then, I guess I've been told. How much longer are you gonna harass me before you show me Linda's office?" She breaks out a smile, giving Jonathan permission to let his own shine again.

"Oh, I can harass you *while* taking you to her office. Two birds, one stone."

Alone inside Linda's office, Regina admits she has no idea what she's looking for. Evidence? She's a preacher, not a P.I. She slumps against the door for a moment in despair. But the only thing that matters now is Jonathan, not her feelings of inadequacy. She straightens her spine and steps back toward Linda's desk.

When Linda's door opens moments later, Regina, already in motion, dashes to the private bathroom in the office and stands behind its partially open door. She focuses on breathing quietly and not moving. Linda enters the office and sets a bag down on the desk. Rolling her neck, she walks toward her bathroom, and Regina prepares to get stone-cold busted.

Linda's phone rings as she puts her hand on the bathroom door. Turning back, she moves to her purse and pulls out her cell phone.

"I told you not to call me on this phone, use the burner... Oh, I dumped it after the murder, that's right. Well, what do you want?" Linda laughs as she listens. "The *last* place we need to be is anywhere near each other right now... No, all *you* need to do is stay calm and this whole thing goes away... Fine, where do you want to meet?" She scribbles something on a notepad and tears the piece of paper off, folding it in half and putting it in her purse. "Just stay calm until I get there, ok?...Bye."

"Men," Linda half sighs and half groans. She puts her purse on her shoulder and walks out, shutting the office door behind her.

Regina hardly has time to exhale. She knows she has got to follow Linda. Grabbing a pencil from the desk, she runs it across the paper underneath the one Linda had written on and stuffs it in her bag. Listening at the door, she opens it and makes her way to the elevators, where she sees the numbers heading down on one. Running to the stairs, she speeds down the floors, praying she can catch up with the elevator on the ground floor.

She takes a moment to collect herself so that she doesn't look like a crazy person when she exits the steps onto the first floor. Looking around, she sees Linda getting into a cab outside and dashes after her. She tries to hail a cab to follow Linda, but they all seem to be ignoring her. What is the secret ingredient needed to hail a cab in New York City? She fumes.

Seeing a bus approaching, she boards. Pulling out the paper she had taken, she takes a moment to decipher it.

"Do you go near 42nd & 9th?" she asks, hoping she is interpreting the markings on the paper correctly.

"Yup, pay up."

"How much?"

The driver just shakes his head and waves her back onto the nearly empty bus. As they ride, Regina remembers to text Jonathan to let him know what she's up to, only to see her phone is dead. Rooting through her bag for a charging brick, she almost misses the driver telling her this is her stop.

Hurrying off the bus, she is too distracted to remember to walk like she knows where she's going and be aware of her surroundings without looking like she's looking. She doesn't notice the man who gets off the bus after her and follows her.

When she comes to her senses a few moments after the bus pulls off, she immediately recognizes she is in a rough part of town. This is not the place for people who have no idea where they are going. She quickens her place and walks toward a few shops up ahead.

Regina can hear two men behind her closing the distance between them and her, despite her quick pace. They overtake her, one man blocking her path forward and one pushing her into the alley.

"Slow down, mama! What's your hurry? You look lost. I'm just trying to help."

Regina is not from New York City, but she's no country bumpkin. She knows they mean her harm. She has put herself in an untenable position.

"Help! Call 911! Help!" she screams at the top of her lungs as she struggles against them not to be forced into the dark alley.

The tall one in front of her pulls out a switchblade, and Regina freezes. "I was just gonna take your money, but when I have to pull my knife, it gets bad for you, see?"

She is pretty sure she's in the kind of neighborhood where, *if* anyone hears her, they will not call for help on a stranger's behalf.

"I have nothing you want, but I have something you need, the salvation of Jesus Christ, and it's free!" She figures if she is about to die, she should go for broke.

The two men actually double over with laughter. That's when the man from the bus who followed her hits one with a trash can and the other with the lid. The knife clatters to the ground. The two men recover and turn on their attacker.

"Who are you, her lover? We're gonna show you what happens when you stick your nose in where it doesn't belong."

Regina tries to snap out of being frozen to help the man. She doesn't know if he's on her side, but he could still save her. Then her jaw drops as he, looking completely cornered, does actual kung-fu magic—at least it seems that way to her—and knocks the two men out cold with kicks to the head.

He turns to Regina and walks slowly over to her. She finally snaps out of being frozen and squares up into a fighting posture, knowing she doesn't stand a chance, but determined not to go down without a fight. The man stops and lifts his hands up.

"Pastor Grant, you offered them Jesus, but *me* you wanna fight?"

"I don't make no sense... wait, you *know* me?"

"Sure. You're my pastor. I'm one of your online members. I joined last year."

"Oh, wow. I'm sorry, I don't remember your face." Regina's body relaxes.

"I always keep my camera off. I'm Charles."

"Oh, yeah, Charles! Ok, now I'm up to speed. Charles, you probably saved my life tonight, and I want to thank you properly, but can we *please* get out of this alley and someplace with lights and people who don't want to murder me?"

"I'm sorry. Of course, let's go."

They walk out of the alley and down the street. He walks even faster than she did when she thought she was walking fast. "So, Charles," she pants, trying to keep up with him, "Why is your camera always off when you log on for our activities?"

His pace slows, then stops as he turns to face her. "Are you kidding me?"

He pulls the hoodie from his head and the street lamps reveal what looks to Regina's eye like burn damage affecting the color and texture of his face. She winces as her heart rate has finally calmed down enough for her to really take him in. She wants to look away but makes herself keep looking until she finds something beautiful in his face.

"I'm sorry that we haven't made the environment loving enough that you thought you wouldn't be welcomed exactly as you are. Sometimes we need help to see the beauty in people. These marks on your face may try to disguise who you are, but who you are can always win out."

"My life experiences haven't borne that out. I *saw* your face when you first really looked at me. You flinched."

"And do you see my face now?"

"Yeah."

"Am I scared of or disturbed by you?"

Charles looks more deeply into her eyes. "No," he

says with surprise.

"I'm still here, entirely because of your awesome kung-fu-pow, by the way, and you've blessed me with the opportunity to stop and *truly* see you, to go beyond what appears and behold what is. I am entirely in your debt and at your mercy. I ask your forgiveness and would like the chance to do better."

"No one's asked me for something in a long time."

"Well, hold on to your hoodie, because I need *one* more favor. Would you give the rest of us at church a chance to really get to know you? Will you put your camera on next time you join us online?" She looks up hopefully at him.

"I'll think about it. That's a promise. Now, how about I get you where you need to be right now?"

"I'll take you up on both of those offers."

As they walk to the subway, a flickering street lamp turns on to illuminate a billboard featuring none other than Captain Seafood. Regina slows and then stops midway through crossing the street to stare at the Captain's face. She feels like she should be remembering something, but she can't quite grab onto it.

"Pastor, you good?" Charles asks.

"What?" She clears her head, caught unawares once again. "Yes, of course. Let's get me out of here!" She hurries along, only looking back once to try to figure out what she was missing.

Dead End

The next morning, she and Jonathan return to where she had been the night before.

"*This*? *Here*? What were you thinking coming here alone, at night, and with no cell phone?!"

"Calm down, nephew, you know I have angels watching over me. Shush, it was fine," she lies. "I'm gonna go in. If I'm not out in fifteen, call the posse."

"Posse?"

"I'm trying out names for our group. What do you think?"

Jonathan rolls his eyes. "It's a good thing you can preach. Fifteen minutes, and then I'm coming in there."

Regina sees a woman going in the side door of the building and enters the same way. She follows the woman upstairs to what looks like a large rehearsal space. Sitting there behind a piano is Roger's friend, Garrett.

She walks up to him and has the joy of seeing his mask of charm slip for a moment.

"Ah, my dear, august woman, how do you do? What brings you to my humble little production, pray tell?"

"What do you and Linda have to talk about on a burner phone after the murder of Archibald Mansfield?" Regina doesn't have time to play around.

"What? Whatever do you mean?"

He had let his mask slip once. She supposes it is too much to hope that he will fold like a house of cards. She had hoped to get *some* kind of sign that she was on the right track.

"Linda came here last night after a frantic call from you. I want to know what you talked about. Were you her little minion, killing Archibald on her behalf?"

Garrett's face blanches. "Murder? I've got nothing to do with anyone's murder. You can't pin that on me."

"I just think all of this will be very interesting to the police."

"I'm not going down for that! It was all her idea!"

Linda steps out from a door Regina hadn't noticed. So much for being a crack observer. "The problem with you men is you're *weak*, no spine to you at all." Gesturing to Regina, she laughs. "She's got *nothing* and already you're about to collapse onto your fainting couch." She looks at Regina, and her expression softens slightly. "I guess it's time for us to come clean. I can see you're not going to let this go."

"No, I'm not." Regina folds her arms and divides a leveling look between the two of them.

Garrett turns to her, all of his charming bravado evaporated. "It takes money to stay on Broadway, well, in my case, anyway. It seemed like such a harmless thing to leak the Captain's potential restaurant locations to his competition. Worse case scenario, he makes a little less money."

"And he would have never known, just chalked it all up to bad luck, if you hadn't gotten greedy!" Linda fumes in his direction.

"I thought the Captain was your friend," Regina looks at Linda, "and *more* to you. You stole from him and killed Archibald over *money*? But you're both already rich."

Linda and Garrett laugh. "No my dear, we're just like you, just poor little hangers-on, depending on the largesse of our betters. And doesn't the Captain just know it every time he summons me, that he can buy me and sell me four times over without even having to take out a line of credit. Garrett has money, but it's not enough. I have some power, but it's not enough. Don't think Roger's any different. They're all the same.

"But one thing you've gotten wrong, my dear, is the only part that won't help you. Yes, we stole from the Captain. But we didn't kill Archibald. I was with the Captain when he was murdered. And..." she gestures to Garrett, who looks as if he's being tortured for information, "Well, you see *he* couldn't kill anyone."

And Regina realizes Linda is right. None of their confessions help Jonathan if they didn't murder Archibald. She was wrong. Linda is a criminal, but not a murderer.

She walks woodenly out of the building and back to the car. Jonathan can tell from her expression that the promising leads have led to nothing. He puts his head on the steering wheel.

"I thought I did everything right! Why is this happening to me?!"

Regina sees the tears rolling down his face. "Why *not* you? The rain falls on the righteous and the wicked alike. The question is, how are you going to *respond*? I don't hear any fat lady singing. Pray to the Lord for strength. And a break in this case, Lord. We could really use that, Father."

"Prayer isn't the answer to everything, you know." Jonathan sits up and wipes the tears from his face.

"I think you and I might define prayer a little differently is all," she says soothingly. "Let's carry this weight together. It will still be heavy, but maybe it will be bearable." She opens up her arms in the car. "Come to Auntie."

Jonathan laughs. "You know I'm not a kid,

right?"

"Really? Because I see a booger hanging from you like some snot-nosed kid, so I'm not so sure." She squeezes his nose and laughs to let out the tension and Jonathan joins in. A long moment of silence visits the car.

"Can I still have that hug?" Jonathan asks bashfully.

"Always." She hugs her nephew and tries not to let her own tears fall as he sheds his in her arms. They have no leads. Although she holds him fiercely in her arms, she feels like he's slipping away.

Detective Simms walks down the marina. His trench coat is wrinkled and there's a spot on his shirt from the blueberry compote at lunch. But that won't stop him from doing what he has to do. He reads the berth numbers as he walks, looking for number 132.

He stops in front of a modest-sized yacht. He has seen some doozies in the Hamptons. This one is actually functional and a proper sailboat, he relishes.

"Hello! Permission to come aboard?"

Nothing stirs in the ship. Looking around, Simms boards the boat. He climbs down to the lower deck and finds a messy and lived-in but spacious and well-appointed bedroom.

"Hold it right there," a voice from behind him barks.

He raises his hands and remains still. "Hold on there, boys, I'm on the job. Just going to reach slowly into my left breast pocket to pull out my ID."

"Nice and slow," the voice behind him instructs.

The officer without a gun trained on Simms' back takes the ID and looks it over, then shows it to his partner, who holsters his weapon.

"Sorry about that. Can't be too careful these days. You on the job? This is a bit out of your jurisdiction, is it not?"

"I'm not *sure* if I'm on the job or not. I got a call saying to come to this berthing address. All they said was that I'd find something interesting. To be honest, I'm not seeing it."

"Sounds like we got the same call." The officers exchange names and handshakes with Simms.

"Well, that's look and see what we find," Simms suggests.

The three fan out to do a circumspect search. They all know they can only take stock of what's out in the open. Anything else won't stick in court. They all look at each other and shake their heads when they find nothing. Simms points upstairs and they emerge from below deck and find nothing else to look for. Simms looks at the bundled main sail and cocks his head.

"Boys, let down that jib, would you?"

"Say what?"

Simms shakes his head. "Kids today." He moves around them to unfurl the jib at the bow of the ship. As the sail raises, a dead body tumbles out from the rigging. This time there is no mistake. Captain Seafood is dead.

All's Well?

"You're free, you're free, you're free!"

Regina can't stop hugging Jonathan, so Ilana turns it into a group hug. Even Roger finds space to clap him on the back and say congratulations.

Finally, they all compose themselves and take a seat at the diner across from the police station, where they've just met with Detective Simms and the assistant district attorney to have the charges dropped.

Ilana and Jonathan talk excitedly now that doom is no longer hanging over them.

"Care to move to another table and give these two a bit of privacy?" Roger smiles warmly at Regina.

"Good idea," she chimes and picks up her cup of lavender mint tea to follow him.

She settles in and takes a sip of her tea, trying to calm down, but the feelings of joy seem to burst out of her. She taps her feet and even contemplates playing the drums with the utensils on the table. Luckily, Roger distracts her.

"Ilana tells me that after Jonathan got arrested, she found you at the train station about to head back to D.C." His eyes are steady on hers. He sees when her gaze turns from one of jubilation to shame.

"That's right," she confesses.

"Without even a call to let me know you're leaving? I feel like a fool." Roger takes a gulp of his coffee and looks away.

Regina reaches out to grab his hand, but then hesitates. He sees that.

"I'm sorry, Roger."

"I didn't think you were the type of woman to lead a man on, Reverend Grant."

"Do you realize you've never just called me Regina? Always Reverend. Why do you think that is?"

"I'm giving you the respect of your title."

Regina grabs his hands and looks into his eyes. "I think you need me as a *pastor*, not a girlfriend, and it's easy to get the two confused. I know you may insist otherwise, but trust me, I've been in this situation a lot more times than you, and I know the signs. You need a fresh spiritual wind in your life, and I represent that to you. Of course you're attracted to me. I look like God.

"I'm sorry it won't turn out the way you wanted, but I think this could be something even better. And I want you to know as your pastor I can see the *real* you, and that's hard to do in a romantic entanglement. No judgment, no expectations. Please trust me, it's better this way."

Roger takes a long look at her.

"It feels true, doesn't it?" she asks when she sees his expression change.

"Maybe," he says grumpily. "I'm not used to being told I'm wrong or being turned down by women."

Regina bristles. "I'm not 'women', I'm *me*." She continues more cheerfully, "And I'm not turning you down, I'm turning you *up*."

Roger shakes his head. "*And* you're corny... but I can't say you're wrong. Did you really mean it? You'll be my pastor?"

"I already am, if you'll let me."

"Been a long time since I had one of those. Well, I've got a day full of meetings, but I was glad I could get away for this."

"Roger, I don't know how to thank you for all you've done for Jonathan. Your lawyer, the bail money, and the support have been a very present help in a time of trouble. We owe you everything. I can't repay you, but I promise to pay it forward as best I can. *Thank you.*"

"It was the least I could do. He was my guest when all of this happened, and I felt responsible. And I knew how much you cared about him. What's money for if you can't help people with it?"

"Indeed."

Roger gives her what she knows is a parting look and reaches out to squeeze her hand. "See you, Pastor." He walks out of the cafe, stopping briefly to shake Jonathan and Ilana's hands, and is gone.

"See you, Roger." Regina puts her head down on the table and tries not to cry.

"Everything ok?" Jonathan asks as he slides into the booth opposite her.

"It will be."

"I know I've been giving you grief about your little romance with him, but I don't *mean* anything by it."

"Young nephew, there are things that go on in my life that have nothing to do with you, believe it or not."

"What is it, then? I thought you two were vibing?"

Regina takes a deep breath in and lets it out slowly. "We *were* vibing, and I liked him very much, but sometimes you have to pick if you're going to be a pastor or a romantic partner."

"You don't have to be *everybody's* pastor. He's not even a member of your church."

"Would that it were that simple, Jonathan. It will be fine, better than fine."

"For everyone but you, it sounds like," Jonathan says regretfully.

"I tell you who's *not* fine, poor Archibald Mansfield and now Captain Seafood," Regina says, changing the topic to less painful matters.

"I can't believe the Captain is dead. It looks like your theory about the killer wanting to kill Archibald was wrong. Someone was after the Captain all along."

"Hmmm," Regina says noncommittally.

"'Hmmm,' what?"

"Just doesn't quite make sense."

"*None* of it makes sense, but I'm certainly glad it's not our problem anymore."

"Hmmm,"

"What's the problem?" Jonathan asks, hearing the tone in Regina's voice.

"Isn't it still our problem? We *knew* Archibald and the Captain."

"Do you think we're caped crusaders or something? Leave some work for the cops."

"Like they've been doing so far? They already tried to pin it on you. The next person could be innocent, too."

"Aunt Regina, I know me being charged with this murder got you involved, but at some point, you are going to have to let this go."

Regina takes a gulp of her now cold lavender mint tea. "I guess you're right. I can't do it all. Besides, I almost forgot this whole trip was supposed to be a vacation. What do you say we celebrate you being free and clear before I head back home?"

"Are you going to make me go to more tea shops?" Jonathan asks suspiciously.

"It's up to you where we go... well, maybe *one* more tea shop if we have time." Regina says hopefully.

That evening, Regina says goodbye to Jonathan and Ilana in the rideshare at the train station before heading inside. She makes it all the way to her correct track and sees the train pull in on time.

She's relieved beyond words that Jonathan is cleared of the murder charges, but she can't stop thinking about how close they seemed to come to losing him. If the investigation charges another innocent person, some other family will have to go through what she did with Jonathan, but it probably won't end so happily.

"All aboard!" the porter shouts. He looks at Regina. "Ma'am, are you boarding?"

"I love a good train ride, but I think I have to try and solve a murder right now." Regina becomes more sure of her decision as she speaks the words.

"Are you a cop?"

"Nope."

"Well, what are you?"

Regina smiles. "I'm a pastor who's gonna get to the bottom of things."

The porter steps on the train as it slowly begins to move. "Good luck!"

Regina picks up her bag and heads out of the tunnels back upstairs. "I'm gonna need it."

Die, Preacher

"This has got to be one of the craziest things you've ever done!" Jonathan walks beside Regina and tries to pull her suitcase out of her hand.

"You were fine when I was doing it for *you*." Regina tightens the grip on her bag and pulls. Almost tipping herself over, but successfully getting her bag out of Jonathan's hands, she keeps walking into the hotel.

"I would have hoped you could understand. The next person to get charged for this crime might not have all the resources we did. I just want to make sure they get the right person, so no one has to go through what you did, or worse!"

Jonathan takes a breath and starts over. "I *get* that you're a compassionate person, but just what are you going to do, go running around the streets of New York after a killer on your own?"

Detective Simms walks in the building and catches Regina's eye, waving a greeting. Jonathan looks back and forth between them.

"Oh, *this* is your partner-in-solving-crime? Didn't they take the case *away* from Mr. Small Town Cop?"

"Jonathan!" She looks disapprovingly at him. "No need to be demeaning."

He takes a deep breath. "Sorry, Detective. I'm grateful for everything you've done. I just mean, with this now involving Captain Seafood, isn't this a little over your head? And *why* involve her? Can't you explain to her this is not a game? She could get hurt!"

Simms looks at him for a moment before speaking, "Son, I can appreciate that you want to take care of your aunt. Believe me, she knows what she's doing, and I will keep her well out of harm's way, I promise. I *was* off of this case, until I found Captain Seafood. Now I'm in charge of the entire investigation. That is why I could push for the dismissal of charges against you."

"That's great that you're in charge again, but you *don't* need my aunt's help. Tell her."

"That's just not true. Rev. Regina has something to contribute to this case. She's been a step ahead of *some* of us from the very beginning. I welcome her help. Like I said, I'll keep her safe."

"You're all *mad*!" Jonathan says in disbelief.

The next morning, Regina meets Detective Simms to touch base.

"I might have a connection with the Captain's wife. *Maybe.* I could try, anyway." Regina waits as the tea bag of ginger oolong she brought from home steeps in the hot water she ordered.

"I'm not having the best of luck with her. Even tried a female officer. She's shut tight, so it's worth a shot." Simms drains his paper coffee cup and throws it in the trash. "I'll walk you back to your motel."

"*Hotel*," Regina corrects.

"As you say."

"It's really not necessary."

"In this neighborhood, it is, especially if I'm going to keep my promise to your nephew." Simms escorts her up the half a block to her building and up to her door. "Don't worry about Jonathan not understanding why you have to see this through. He doesn't get that you and I are built differently."

"*Are* we?" Regina leans back to let the conversation play out.

"You know we are. Neither one of us are superheroes, but when we really see something, we can't unsee it. You witnessed firsthand how a criminal investigation can swiftly and unjustly ensnare the innocent.. Now you're compelled to see this case closed without that happening again."

She stands stunned for a minute. "Wow. Thanks for understanding me better than I understand myself. What did *you* see that won't let you rest on this case?"

Simms thinks for s moment, then frowns. "Something's just not right. We're missing major pieccs of the puzzle here. Once I start to put the pieces together, I *have* to see it through to the end."

Regina unlocks her room door and picks up the piece of paper that must have been stuffed underneath. She freezes midway into standing back up and the door she had swung open crashes back into her. Simms looks over her shoulder to read what's on the paper that has her frozen. In large, block, hand printed letters it reads "Die, Preacher."

He immediately puts a hand forward to hold open the door. "Stand up and step away from the door," he commands. He walks inside the room, making sure no one else is there. Coming back out, he looks at the paper in her hand and pulls out a plastic glove and a plastic bag from his coat's pocket.

"I'll take that." His gloved hand takes the paper, puts it in the plastic bag and seals it. "I'll call a unit over to dust the door for prints. Maybe the inside, too. You're going to have to move, seeing as *someone* knows where you are. Have you got a place to go?"

Regina walks into a suite of rooms at the Hilton. "The Holiday Inn would have been fine, but I can't exactly say I mind."

Roger follows behind her after tipping the doorman who carried her bag. "Well, I disagree with *what* you're doing, but you shouldn't have your life threatened because of it. And you *know* that place you were staying at was sketchy to begin with. I'm happy you asked for help in relocating."

Regina is too tired to disagree with him about the sketchiness of her accommodations. "Well, that's great," she says woodenly. "I'm going to get some rest now. See you later."

It takes her a while to notice that he is not moving.

"*Goodbye,*" she repeats, only to see him continue to stand there. "Is there a problem?"

"Oh, I'm not going anywhere," he says definitively.

"Excuse me?"

"You don't get to tell me you have a death threat and you need help changing hotels and then expect me to disappear. I'm not letting you out of my sight." He crosses his arms in emphasis.

"Is this a *man* thing?"

"I think it's a reasonable human being thing but, yes, if you need it to be, it's a *man* thing."

Regina rolls her eyes. "Well, you're sleeping on the couch."

Roger laughs. "I bought out the floor. Don't worry, I won't crowd you."

Regina opens her mouth but then closes it before she says any of the things she has planned. Of course, he knows how expensive it is and he doesn't care. He has more important things to do, but he's so important that those other things will wait for him to be available.

And he knows she can take care of herself, except for this situation where she needs some help.

"Thanks. I appreciate you."

"No chance I can get you to change your mind and just let this whole thing go?" Roger asks hopefully.

"Oh, it's way too late for that now. I'm going to catch this killer."

"What if you don't? Plenty of murders go unsolved every day. Are you prepared for that possibility?"

"I know that you and Jonathan are trying to keep me safe and to keep me from getting my hopes up, but you've got to understand that I *live* in hope, so it's impossible to avoid it with me. I'm built to believe I can make a difference, so I always have to try."

"You can't fix *everything*."

"But when it lands right in my lap, I have to try! Why does no one understand me?" Regina gets a hold of herself before she delivers a tirade on justice and collective responsibility. No one likes a sanctimonious lecture. Taking a deep breath, she lets go of her need to be right. "I know I can't fix everything, but I'm determined to fix *something*."

All's Well

Three days later, Regina admits she has done all that she can. There are no more leads to run down, no more cages to rattle. The entire investigation had ground to a halt. At least no one seemed to be interested in arresting just *anyone* for the murders. She looks at Roger and Jonathan talking in her suite's living room as she chops vegetables for her famous garden marinara in the kitchen.

She grimaces. It has felt too good to play house these last few days with Roger. If things were a little different... but Regina knows she hasn't read the situation wrong—he belongs in her flock, not her arms, however well he might fit there.

"Earth to Auntie," Jonathan calls as he waves his hands in the air to catch her attention.

She puts down the knife and walks over to them. "It's time for me to go home."

"What? I thought you were going to solve the murder?" Jonathan is more confused than relieved.

"I can't." Regina opens her hands and holds them out in front of her. "I've got nothing. I know I fought to stay here, but I'm big enough to admit when I'm beat. And besides, there are some things at home I need to deal with, no matter how much I'd like to run away from them. No time like the present, so I'll head back tonight."

"You'll have to excuse me if I have whiplash," Jonathan says.

"You know I don't let the grass grow beneath my

feet."

"But you'll be back, right?" Roger asks.

Regina lets out a rich laugh. "You haven't heard the last of me, don't worry!"

Jonathan gets out of the rideshare and walks with Regina to her train's tunnel.

"Spit it out," she says, still looking out across the train tracks.

"I was really scared. Thanks for being there for me. I needed it."

She gives him a fierce hug he gladly returns. Parting, they both wipe tears from their eyes.

"Go on, get out of here. You can release me on my own recognizance, you know."

"What?"

"I know you and the rest of the world want to make sure I get on this train and *really* leave town. I'm getting on the train, I promise."

"Maybe Great Aunt Fay *did* ask me to make sure I saw you safely home," Jonathan admits.

"How did the rest of the world get to be my minder?"

"We just care about you, is all."

"Look, here's the train," Regina says as the train slows on the platform. "You can actually watch me get on."

They share another hug and Regina boards, waiting for the train's crew to switch over. She sees a porter heading her way she recognizes.

"If it isn't the crime-fighting pastor. Did you nab your bad guy?" He jokes.

"I wish I *had*," Regina laughs. She supposes it was a little silly to think she could just snap her fingers and solve a murder.

"By the way, a Mr. Carman is going to meet you at the Hartford, CT stop. He tried to meet you the last time you had a reservation, but you never made it on the train."

"What does he want with me?"

"Something about a job interview for someplace that's all initials."

"Oh, of course! I forgot all about that. Did you say it was a *Mr.* Carman?"

"Yeah. Why?"

Regina pauses as her mind races. Finally, she stands up and pulls her suitcase down from the overhead storage.

"I gotta get off this train. Thanks for your help."

"But what do you want me to tell Mr. Carman?" he asks to the air as he watches her hurry down the walkway.

"Welcome back, Mr. Moile," Eunice says perfunctorily. "I was beginning to wonder when I'd see you again."

"Now that I've seen Rev. Grant off, I can get back to my usual routine." Roger can't decide if he's happy about Regina leaving.

"Rev. Grant hasn't left," Eunice informs him.

"No, this time she has. Her nephew saw her off."

"She called me an hour ago asking for your address in the East Hamptons. Said she was afraid she had forgotten something."

"East Hamptons?! That's the *last* place I want her. Tell Ruiz to fire up the jet. I guess I'm returning to Chez Moile a lot sooner than expected."

*

Roger walks through Chez Moile but doesn't find Regina. The staff don't report having seen her. He exhales. He must have overreacted. When he looks out his patio door to the pool, he doesn't have to focus on the figure dimly lit from the pool lights to know who it is.

He steps out of his doors and walks over to face her. As he moves outside, the area lights around the pool area illuminate.

"Automatic lights," Regina says. "I remembered you told me that. No one would have mistaken poor Archibald for the Captain in this light, no matter how he was dressed. Whoever killed him meant to."

"You shouldn't be here, Rev. Grant."

"The night of the party, you said it was a woman calling who wanted to interview me, but *Mr.* Carman was set to interview me. That was Archibald Mansfield on the phone then. You lied to me."

"I tried to get you to leave this alone."

"You *promised* Jonathan would get exonerated of the murder charges. We were at a dead end, then the Captain shows up dead, clearing Jonathan. Did you kill your friend, the Captain?"

"I couldn't see that young man go to prison for a crime he didn't commit. I had to make it right."

"It occurs to me you make it right by confessing the truth, not by killing more people. Am I right the Captain wasn't your first victim, Archibald was?"

Roger puts a hand to his head as if he's checking for a fever. "Depending on who you ask, there are a lot more victims than that."

"The building that collapsed?" Regina can't imagine how that weighs on him.

"I didn't tell you the entire story. My two

business partners set me up, made it look like *I* had bought substandard materials when all the time it had been them. I was found guilty of 12 counts of manslaughter and sentenced to 72 years in prison.

"Ten years into my sentence, I escaped, rebuilt my life and achieved even greater fortunes. That was almost 20 years ago. I had gotten used to living my life without the faintest hint of suspicion. Money minimizes the questions. Archibald recognized me."

"So you killed him?"

"Do you know what prison is like? I won't go back. This time, there's no way out." His voice is dark and grave.

Regina looks at Roger. He could easily overpower her with his pinky finger. The pool separates them, but he is closest to the only way to get out. She would have to be lucky to slip by him. Maybe this is how she dies.

"No way out... for you or for me?"

She sees mixed emotions pass across his face and realizes he is deciding whether to kill her right in that moment. Regina locks her knees to keep them from shaking. She won't beg.

She should scream at the top of her lungs. Perhaps one of the staff in the house might hear her, but she is rooted to the spot, unable to move or think.

Roger sees she is afraid of him and softens.

"Come here." He gestures to her, but she can't move.

Walking over to her side of the pool, Roger stands behind her and puts his hands on her shoulders. 'This is it,' Regina thinks, 'he is going to drown me.' She means to take a deep breath, but her nerve collapses and she cries instead.

"I'm so sorry it's come to this," Roger says solemnly as he squeezes her shoulders, a little too hard.

"No," she sobs as she shakes under his grip.

"I could never harm you. You're my light in the darkness... Will you help me? Help me turn myself in?"

Regina feels lightheaded with relief, but still shakes herself free of his grip. She doubles over and gasps for air. Now, her tears are from mixed emotions. Somewhere inside, this killer is also a kind man, and she has an idea of what happens to kind men in prison.

Ever So Humble

"Good morning, Ms. Pring," Regina calls as she tries to speed past the admin offices and into her study.

"Gallivanting around New York City when you need to be here trying to keep your church," Ms. Pring scolds as she catches up to her. She is fast.

"I promise, I kept the gallivanting to a minimum, Ms. Pring."

"Shh," Ms. Pring cuts her off on her way to her study. "John Mathews is in there waiting for you. You had better have a good reason for missing church Sunday with no advance notice. It's like you're doing his job *for* him."

Regina sighs. "I guess today's my day of reckoning, then." She takes a swig of the maple green tea in her travel mug, braces herself, then heads into her study.

Dr. Mathews sits in the armchair of her study like a cat welcoming a mouse into its lair. As soon as she walks in, he lays into her. "I can't *wait* to hear what's kept you away from the church for an entire week and a half. I at least thought you cared."

"I know you're here to tell us you took some fancy job in New York. I hear things. How dare you go shopping for another job instead of being here to do the one you have?"

Regina puts her bag down, takes a seat, and thinks about what's been dropped into her lap. "I'm not going anywhere. None of those developments were my doing, and I now know that wealth doesn't suit me."

She takes a deep breath and continues. "I think it's time to start a prison ministry."

"What?" Dr. Mathews does a double-take.

"I thought I could keep people out of jail, but the imprisoned may always be with us. The Lord told us to visit those in prison, to care about their wellbeing like we do our own. I have failed at that so far, but when life lands in your lap, you have to respond.

"There's people in there who need the hope that we can provide. Maybe they could use a pastor. Maybe I could use *them*. It often turns out that the one who is giving actually receives the most. It will be a hard sell for the congregation. I know we're a very comfortable church that might be hesitant to get involved in the thornier issues in life, but it is something that I'm going to do. Hopefully, the church will join in on it with me."

Mathews remained silent for a long time. "My older son is doing a bid in federal prison."

"Sherman? No, I just saw him."

"Not Sherman, Jeremiah. We don't talk about him and few people even remember him around here. He was involved in a robbery where the owner was murdered. He is, in part, responsible for taking a life. I'm so ashamed of him. I'll never forgive him for ruining everything."

"That's not how you really feel. I can see it in your eyes."

Mathews tears up. "My boy is where I can't protect him. I feel so driven to succeed in business so I can give him a *job* when he gets out, to actually have something to help him."

"And I'm standing in the way of that by not changing the time of service to accommodate your business. You're doing all you can for your son." Regina sighs as the genesis of the whole conflict comes into focus. "Dr. Mathews, why didn't I know about Jeremiah until now? Why don't many people remember him around here?"

"The shame! I thought my family would never live it down. It just got to be easier not to mention him, even here."

"Let's change that. Let's change keeping secrets and hurts into supporting one another. It would be great if we could give Jeremiah a church to come home to, one that won't look away. Will you help me start this prison ministry?"

Mathews takes a long look at her. "Yes. It was going to be harder to get you fired than I thought. Turns out people like you. That doesn't mean that I will go any easier on you. We still don't see eye to eye."

Regina smiles. "I'll take what I can get."

"I've never heard you mention a prison ministry before. What brings this up?"

Her smile falters. "You're not the only one with someone you love there."

I hope you enjoyed this book and I look forward to bringing you the rest of the series.

If you would like to keep up with my latest works, I invite you to visit my website at
www.ngozitrobinson.com
where you can also sign up for my mailing list to get sneak peeks of current and future works and insight into my writing process.

www.ingramcontent.com/pod-product-compliance
Lightning Source LLC
Chambersburg PA
CBHW070343130626
46556CB00007B/3007